Lingering Echoes

GHOSTS OF ORDINARY OBJECTS

Lingering Echoes

ANGIE SMIBERT

BOYDS MILLS PRESS
AN IMPRINT OF HIGHLIGHTS
Honesdale, Pennsylvania

To Anita, my favorite aunt, second mother,
and family researcher

Text copyright © 2019 by Angie Smibert

Boyds Mills Press
An Imprint of Highlights
815 Church Street
Honesdale, Pennsylvania 18431
boydsmillspress.com
Printed in the United States of America

ISBN: 978-1-62979-851-6 (hc)
978-1-68437-624-7 (eBook)
Library of Congress Control Number: 2018962589

First edition
10   9   8   7   6   5   4   3   2   1

Design by T. L. Bonaddio
The text of this book is set in Adobe Garamond Pro.
The titles are set in Aviano Sans.

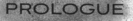

PROLOGUE

THE PARSONAGE WAS closed up tighter than a pickle jar. The lace curtains were drawn over every pane of glass. And the single blue star in the little window over the door was the only thing that cried out to the world.

Aunt Mattie had hung the star after Uncle Henry left for the war. He joined up to be an army chaplain. Yesterday, a uniformed man in a big black sedan had told Aunt Mattie the preacher was never coming back.

Bone tucked the pounding box under her left arm and knocked on the door. The box was growing heavier by the second. A pound of coffee. A pound of beans. A pound of flour. A pound of this. A pound of that. It was what folks in Big Vein did when someone got hurt in the mines or lost a loved one. Across the top of the box lay Mama's butter-yellow sweater, newly mended and full of stories that needed airing. It was the heaviest burden Bone carried, and she needed to share it with Aunt Mattie.

Bone's fist hung in the air. She could still taste the iron-cold bathwater and feel her aunt's hand holding her under. She shivered. The blue star stared back at her. All Bone could see was poor Uncle Henry at the bottom of the ocean, under fathoms of icy water. She knocked one more time.

The lace moved in the window, and the door opened a crack. Bone held her breath.

Ruby slipped through, closing the door softly behind her. Her cousin wiped her hands on the apron she wore over her store-bought dress. It was one of the old, ugly ones she'd given Bone when Mattie threw out almost all her clothes. Ruby had a smudge of flour on her cheek, and her eyes were puffy.

Bone let out the breath, frankly relieved. She wasn't ready to see her aunt. Not really.

"Mother isn't receiving visitors." Ruby's face was tight, like she was pinching off everything bottled up inside of her.

Bone felt her own face tighten, too. It hadn't been easy to knock on that door. The least Aunt Mattie could do was show her face.

"Sorry," Ruby whispered. "She should apologize. She nearly killed you." Then she choked out the next words with a little sob—"It's Daddy"—before catching herself and pushing all those feelings back down.

Bone and Ruby had never been that close, not until recently at least, but that little sob about broke Bone's heart. "I know," she whispered. She set the box down on the porch and hugged her cousin. Bone knew about losing a parent, even if she'd only been six when Mama died. "Take the pounding box."

Ruby wiped her eyes on her apron. As she stooped down to pick up the box, Bone grabbed the sweater off the top. Aunt Mattie wasn't ready to hear its story, and Bone certainly wasn't going to part with it. "See you at church," Bone said quietly.

Ruby nodded. Uncle Henry's funeral was tomorrow. She slipped back inside and closed the door.

Bone hugged her butter-yellow sweater to her chest and breathed in the lavender her mother had always worn. The sweater had been Mama's, and Bone saw its memories. It was her Gift, her useless Gift. She caught a flash of a younger Mama pounding on a door, calling out Mattie's name to no avail.

Some folks never changed.

Why had Bone bothered?

She pulled the sweater on and stomped off home.

An ember of something kindled deep inside her as the leaves crunched under her feet.

October 1942
BIG VEIN, VIRGINIA

1

THE LEAVES WERE as bright as Jack o'lanterns. The crisp air tasted of ghost stories and candy apples and bonfires. Bone Phillips loved this time of year. And she was determined nothing would spoil it. Not the war. Not her daddy being called up. Not the sugar rationing. Not the Gift. And, least of all, not her Aunt Mattie.

Bone felt a twinge of guilt for that last thought. Uncle Henry's funeral had been only last week. But it was Ruby she felt sorry for, mostly.

Stepping off the back porch of the boardinghouse and onto the gravel road that led to school, Bone caught sight of two of the Little Jewels—Pearl and Opal—leaving the parsonage yard. Alone. The boys had started calling them the Little Jewels at the beginning of the school year. And it had stuck. Pearl, Opal, and Ruby went everywhere together. Until now. Pearl and Opal cast a glance back toward the parsonage before trudging toward school.

The first bell rang.

Bone took off running. She skidded to a stop in front of the parsonage, outside the perfect white picket fence. It was supposed to be Ruby's first day back to school after the funeral. The curtains were still pulled tight, but now a little banner with a single gold star outlined in blue hung in the window. For Uncle Henry. It was like autumn had come for the star, turning it golden. Would it change to fire and rust and fall to the ground come winter? Would others fall, too? Almost every house in Big Vein had a blue star, including the boardinghouse. Uncle Henry had gone down with his ship in the North Atlantic. Daddy might be heading across soon, too. She hadn't heard from him in nine days. Mamaw said it was to be expected, but Bone still had nightmares about him being lost somewhere. Not in the ocean, like Uncle Henry. In her dreams, Daddy was wandering through deep, dark foreign woods at night with not even a lantern to light his way home.

Bone shook off the dream. *Ruby was going to school, whether she liked it or not.* Flinging open the gate, Bone marched right up to the front door of the parsonage. Raising her hand to knock, she hesitated. The gold star stared back at her. Without thinking, Bone touched the glass between her and the star—and immediately snatched her hand back. The star was nearly as scalding as a canning jar straight out of the pot, even through the windowpane. She saw a flash of Aunt Mattie crumpling as the army man handed her a folded flag and the gold star. It called to Bone. She took a deep breath and gingerly touched the glass again. This time, she saw Ruby carefully pressing the gold star over the blue one on the banner. The new star was smaller, and Ruby gritted her teeth as she eyeballed placing it exactly in the center.

"*Don't bother with that,*" Aunt Mattie yelled at Ruby.

"*Daddy was a hero,*" Ruby replied quietly.

"*He left us to save strangers.*" Mattie threw the words at Ruby like daggers. Uncle Henry, an army chaplain, had given his life preserver to a sailor when their ship was sunk by a Nazi U-boat. Uncle Henry went down with the ship.

Ruby closed her eyes and took it as Aunt Mattie kept hollering at her. She drew in a deep breath and finished pressing down the edges of the star. The blue border was perfectly even all the way around the gold. Ruby hung up the star dry-eyed before spinning on her heel, stomping across the floor, and slamming her bedroom door. On the outside, Ruby was like the icy water of the Atlantic, but on the inside, she was boiling like a kettle. Bone traced the perfect edges of the star with her finger.

Aunt Mattie was making it real hard to forgive her.

The lace moved a little in the window, startling Bone. Ruby shot out the front door. "Is that what you're wearing?" Ruby looked Bone up and down with a scowl. Ruby, of course, was wearing one of her spotless store-bought dresses. This one was a pretty blue-checked one with a tiny red belt. The outfit reminded Bone of Dorothy's in *The Wizard of Oz*. The only thing missing were the ruby slippers.

"Yes, I am." Bone was wearing her dungarees to school. She also had on a white shirt, boots, and her mother's yellow sweater. These and a pair of corduroy trousers were about all she had left. Aunt Mattie had given away the feedsack dresses Mrs. Price had made for Bone plus the rest of her old clothes when Bone had briefly moved in with the Alberts. Bone wasn't about to wear Ruby's castoffs if she didn't have to. And nobody said she had to anymore. "Hurry up, slowpoke," she hollered as she took off up the road.

Before long, Bone heard the sound of Ruby's shoes running behind her. Together they sped past the church and all the graying clapboard houses huddled along the gravel road up to the mine. It was less than a quarter mile from one end of the coal camp to the school. But it felt good to run like they were still little kids. Soon they caught up with the Little Jewels. Bone half expected Ruby to fall in beside her best friends since first grade, but she raced around them. Bone scrambled to keep up with her.

Ruby was laughing as they collapsed onto one of the picnic tables outside the little two-room schoolhouse.

"Why didn't you want to walk with Pearl and Opal?" Bone asked, panting.

The smile slid off Ruby's face. She shrugged. "I get tired of them being so nice and sweet all the time, telling me to smile like

I got nothing to be mad at." Ruby's fingers dug into the splintery wood plank of the table. "I get the same from folks at church. *Smile, your daddy wouldn't want you sad.*" Ruby imitated one of the elders. "*Don't frown, young lady. Your daddy was a hero.*"

Bone nodded. Folks were always telling her how young ladies were supposed to act or feel. Usually, it was Aunt Mattie doing the telling. "You got every right to be mad," Bone told Ruby. Bone was mad, too. At Aunt Mattie. Uncle Henry, though, was a hero. Bone wasn't quite sure why Ruby was mad at him.

Opal and Pearl walked by without looking at Ruby or Bone.

"That was an interesting turn of events," a voice said from behind them. It was Jake Lilly, and beside him, as usual, was Clay Whitaker. *The boys*, as Bone thought of them, always together.

"Aren't you supposed to be at work?" Bone asked. The two of them had left school not long ago for the mine. They worked outside with Jake's daddy sorting coal and running the mantrip. Clay's father worked down below with Uncle Junior and Bone's best friend, Will. The boys were not wearing their bank clothes—the coveralls all miners wore. Instead, they were dressed in dungarees and sweaters. Each had a sack lunch in one hand and a composition book in the other.

"Mama put her foot down," Clay answered. Jake nodded. "Plus, I think they got some money from the government on account of Carmen and Cliff."

Clay's older brothers had died in the war. Two gold stars hung in the Whitakers' front window.

"Daddy says we can still help out on Saturdays, if we want," Jake added. He didn't look too keen on the idea, though.

Clay shook his head. "Naw, I seen enough coal." Not one month ago Clay had been desperate to help out his family. Now he looked positively relieved to be back at school.

"Me, too." Jake punched Clay in the arm.

Miss Austin rang the bell again. She taught the younger children in the other room of the schoolhouse. The little kids followed her into their room. The older kids filed into Miss Johnson's room, fifth graders sitting in the front, seventh in back.

Bone felt like hugging those boys. They were more fun to have around than the Jewels. The boys dashed to their old spots along the back row. Bone sank into her usual desk, right in front of Jake and Clay. Ruby wavered between sitting next to Bone or the Little Jewels and Robbie Matthews, the mine superintendent's son. Opal had set her bag in Ruby's seat. Ruby had done the same thing to prevent Bone from sitting with them at the beginning of the school year. Opal relented, though, and moved her bag. Ruby smiled wanly at Bone. "I better make nice," she mouthed before she sat next to her friends.

Bone felt the familiar jab of pencil lead between her shoulder blades.

"We sure have missed your stories, Bone," Jake said.

"Yeah, we need a good ghost story," Clay agreed. "At lunch."

Bone smiled. Things were getting back to normal, even if Will was still down in the mines. "Did I ever tell you the one about Stingy Jack?" she whispered. "It's the tale about the Jack o'lanterns."

"No!" Clay leaned in, clearly hungry for more.

"Granddaddy calls them Jack ma lanterns," Jake said.

"So does Mamaw!" Bone knew he wasn't talking about the carved pumpkins that sat out on folks' porches on Halloween. Jack ma lanterns were what a lot of the older folks called ghost lights. They were the tiny lights that floated around in the woods on a dark and scary night. But the Jack o'lanterns and ghost lights all came from the same story about Stingy Jack.

Miss Johnson cleared her throat and glared in their direction.

"I love Halloween," Jake threw in one last poke.

"Me, too," Bone whispered. She really did. This year Bone wanted to be a witch like the bad one in *The Wizard of Oz*. Mrs. Price was going to make her a hat and cape for the carnival. She was a whiz with her Singer sewing machine. Maybe the boys could be her flying monkeys. Or Will could be the Tin Man.

"We're so glad to have Miss Albert back with us," Miss Johnson said, motioning everyone to settle down.

Ruby slunk low in her seat.

"And Mr. Whitaker and Mr. Lilly," Miss Johnson added.

The boys straightened up, actually beaming at everyone. It was an interesting turn of events. They hadn't ever exactly loved school.

"Before we get started, though, I've got an unfortunate announcement to make."

All eyes snapped to the front, and the room fell silent.

Was it Daddy? If it were, an army man would've come to the boardinghouse—just like they'd come to the parsonage and to the Whitakers'. Bone glanced around. No one seemed to be missing. It could be the father or brother of one of the little ones in the other room, though.

"This year's Halloween carnival has been canceled." Miss Johnson folded her hands in front of her and waited for a reaction.

Bone (and everyone around her) let out their breath. No one had died. But then again, no Halloween carnival? It was always at the church hall on Halloween. Everyone dressed up in costumes, bobbed for apples, ate themselves sick on candy, and told ghost stories.

"No!" several fifth graders exclaimed.

"Why?" Bone let out a whine.

"Sugar!" Jake exclaimed. He meant it as a swear. Bone felt like saying worse.

"Yes, Mr. Lilly, sugar," Miss Johnson answered. She did not mean it as a swear. "The carnival is canceled because of sugar rationing—and because a certain community member doesn't think it's appropriate to celebrate this holiday." Miss Johnson did not look at Ruby as she said this, but everyone else did.

Ruby slunk down in her seat as far as she could go.

Aunt Mattie was notorious for thinking things were not appropriate. Not Bone's clothes. Not her running around with Will or Jake and Clay. Not the Gift. Now not Halloween. The preacher's wife had often remarked on Halloween being the devil's night or a heathen holiday. *She wants everyone to be as miserable as she is.* Bone could still hear fabric ripping as Aunt Mattie jerked the sweater clean off Bone's back. She could still feel her aunt's bony grip as she dragged her down the hall. She could still taste the iron-cold water as Aunt Mattie plunged her head under. Bone's insides smoldered.

Bone closed her eyes so that all she could see was that darn gold star. Uncle Henry, she told herself. Aunt Mattie was grieving Uncle Henry. Bone tamped down her anger.

Miss Johnson let the clamor go on for a few seconds before she motioned for everyone to settle down. "I know everyone will find a safe and fun way to celebrate All Hallows' Eve."

The boys groaned.

Miss Johnson turned to pick up the books that were on her desk. "But now we're going to talk about . . ."

Jake poked Bone again. "Oh, we'll find a safe and fun way to celebrate. I got us an idea for a prank."

Clay nodded sagely. "If there ain't no treats, we'll put the tricks back into Halloween all right." He had a devilish gleam in his eye.

Bone turned back to the front and crossed her arms. Halloween used to be all about the tricks. Her Uncle Ash had told her about pranks he and Junior and Mama played when they were kids. Usually, they involved removing someone's gate or stealing a mailbox. Some of the pranks were even on Aunt Mattie, like the time Ash and Junior locked her in the outhouse. No wonder she doesn't like Halloween. Bone suppressed a grin as Miss Johnson handed a miserable Ruby a book.

"Seventh graders, I'm handing out books for you to write reports on." She gave Opal, Pearl, and Robbie books. Each one looked different.

Jake and Clay groaned again, but Bone sat up. She loved book reports, especially if she hadn't read the story before. Even if she had. Miss Johnson was always talking about the Brontë sisters. Was it maybe *Wuthering Heights*? Bone had seen the movie last summer when the mine showed it outside. A servant boy falls in love with a rich girl on the dark moors of England. It was spooky and thrilling yet a bit sappy. Bone strained to look at the cover of the book Miss Johnson was about to hand her. As she took it eagerly, Miss Johnson winked at her. "This one is my favorite."

A thrill went through Bone, part anticipation, part something else. Touching the book Miss Johnson lovingly placed in her hands, Bone could feel the warm crackle of a fire and smell woodsmoke. Bone closed her eyes. Bathed in orange firelight, a young Miss Johnson curled up next to the hearth reading this book. The hunger in her to be like the person described in these pages still radiated off its cover. Bone felt that same feeling when she read a good book. She'd so wanted to be Dorothy or Alice living in a magical land. Bone opened her eyes and read the title. *The Life of Charlotte Brontë*. Bone felt the thrill go right out of her.

"As you'll notice, these are biographies, and each of you got a different one. Opal, what's a biography?"

It was a true story about a person. Everyone knew that. And Bone didn't like true stories. Bone loved to read and tell *stories*. About Gypsy curses and ghosts and devil dogs and Jack and Ashpet. Not about real things that happened. Her Gift was all about seeing real things that had happened to objects, or at least to the people who owned them—and she still didn't like it one little bit.

Bone placed the book on her desk and crossed her arms again. As she did, her fingers brushed across Mama's butter-yellow sweater.

Mama was watching Bone go off to school the first time. Will held her hand tightly while she jabbered on about some story. He was two years older but had been held back on account of not talking. Bone felt Mama's mix of love, pride, and sadness as the pair plodded up the road. Mama followed them all the way to the schoolhouse without them noticing.

Her Gift was not entirely useless, Bone conceded. It had given her back pieces of Mama—bits she knew, bits she didn't know, even how she died.

Mama being gone was Aunt Mattie's fault.

Usually, Bone got an icy cold feeling in her stomach when she thought of Aunt Mattie holding her head under that freezing bathwater. Now an ember of fury warmed her belly.

Miss Johnson went on about the differences between biography and autobiography, but Bone didn't hear any of it—until Jake poked her in the back again with a slightly less sharp pencil. He handed her a note. *Let's egg a certain community member's house come Halloween.*

Miss Johnson cleared her throat.

Bone hid the note under the book. She tried to listen as Miss Johnson moved on to history and then math. But all she could think about was what the sweater had showed her a few weeks ago. Mama had been nursing Aunt Mattie during the influenza outbreak. This one hadn't been as bad as the one in 1918 that had killed millions. In 1936, several people hereabouts had died. But when Aunt Mattie nearly died, Willow Reed Phillips laid her hands on her sister and cured her. That was Mama's Gift. She could see what was wrong with people and heal them. Only healing Mattie took all Mama's energy, and she couldn't heal herself. Mama died saving Aunt Mattie. If only Mama hadn't . . . Bone took a deep breath and pushed down that thought, screwing the lid on tight, hoping that would snuff out the ember in her gut.

The lunch bell rang.

Bone crammed the note inside *The Life of Charlotte Brontë* and stuffed both in her desk.

"You owe her for what she done to you," Clay whispered as they grabbed their sack lunches. Aunt Mattie had tried to baptize the Gift right out of Bone, nearly drowning her in the process.

Bone nodded, her insides broiling, but then she watched Ruby as they all filed out to the picnic tables. Ruby dragged behind her friends as if her sack lunch weighed a thousand pounds. Bone shook her head. "Ruby don't deserve that—neither does Uncle Henry."

Clay stared at his feet. "Guess you're right."

"Damn, I hadn't thought about Ruby or the preacher," Jake said. "Okay, Bone. We'll think of something else." He and Clay exchanged a glance.

The three of them settled down at the picnic table under the sugar maple. Bright orange leaves fluttered onto the pine tabletop. Bone brushed them aside. She laid out an apple and her fried bologna sandwich wrapped neatly in wax paper. The bologna was black and crispy, just how she liked it. Jake unwrapped two pieces of fried chicken and handed one to Clay. He only had two butter biscuits and a small jelly jar in his sack. He slid a biscuit over to Jake.

"How about a ghost story, then?" Clay asked, tearing his biscuit and slathering it with a huge dollop of apple butter. "A good and scary one."

"That would lift my spirits!" Jake laughed at his own joke. "Get it?"

Clay groaned loudly. "That one about Stingy Jack."

Bone grinned. There wasn't anything she loved better than telling a good story. "Once there was a stingy old man named Jack. He was a blacksmith. And he loved to play tricks on people—"

"Damn, Bone, I missed these stories," Jake interrupted.

Clay nodded, his mouth full of biscuit.

"It's awful boring sorting coal with nobody but this lunk for company." Jake elbowed Clay. "Y'all come listen. Bone's telling a good 'un." He waved over the rest of the seventh grade with his drumstick.

"Ha, ha," Clay said, his mouth slightly less full. "Shut up, and let her tell the blame story."

Pearl and Opal eagerly slid in beside Jake, and Ruby sat by Bone. Robbie leaned against the tree munching an apple. They were all that was left of the seventh grade. A few sixth graders turned around in their seats to listen.

"One fine day, the devil called on Jack. He'd disguised himself as an old man, but Jack was no fool. He knew the devil had come to collect his soul. But ole Jack tricked him." Bone took a bite of her bologna sandwich and chewed as she considered which version of the story to tell. Stingy Jack had vexed the devil with his sheer orneriness in a number of ways. She settled on the simplest one. "Stingy Jack agreed to go if the devil bought him a drink first. The devil turned himself into a nickel to pay for the drink, but Jack stuffed that coin in his pocket next to a little silver cross he carried. The devil was stuck, right there in Jack's pocket as a plug nickel, until Old Scratch agreed to leave without Jack's soul and not come back for ten years."

"That was right smart," Clay said. Others nodded.

"The devil kept his word and didn't come back for a whole decade," Bone continued. She told them all about how Jack tricked the devil again and again—until he was a very old man. By the time Bone got to the best part of the story, all of the sixth and fifth grade had gathered around. "When it came time for Jack to die, though, neither Saint Peter nor the devil wanted him."

Ruby was wide-eyed. "What'd he do?"

"Well, that's what Jack asked the devil. What was he supposed to do? It was so dark and cold out in the world." Bone paused for effect. Everyone leaned in. "The devil fetched Jack an ember from the fires of eternal damnation itself. He told old Jack to go make his own hell on earth." Bone whispered *hell* so the teacher couldn't hear her swear.

Ruby and the Little Jewels gasped—and then tittered.

"So Jack carved out a pumpkin and stuck that ember in it. He carried it like a lantern, roaming the night between heaven and hell. And folks say you can see him still, especially on Halloween night, wandering the deep, dark woods."

"Oh, that's where we get the Jack o'lantern!" one of the fifth graders cried out in delight.

Bone breathed in the crisp, fall air. Sunlight streamed through the orange and red leaves of the sugar maple overhead. A single gold leaf drifted down and landed on the picnic table in front of her.

2

IN THE BOARDINGHOUSE parlor, President Roosevelt's voice crackled over the radio: "There are millions of Americans in army camps, in naval stations, in factories, and in shipyards . . ." Uncle Ash's fox terrier, Corolla, wiggled into Bone's lap as she sat cross-legged by the hearth. Uncle Junior leaned forward in Daddy's chair. Bone missed the smell of Daddy's cherry tobacco, the smoke curling up to the ceiling. Mamaw, Mrs. Price, and Miss Johnson were perched on the settee. Mrs. Price's knitting needles clicked away as Uncle Ash paced and smoked behind them all.

Mr. Roosevelt had been having these fireside chats on the radio for as long as Bone could remember. Of course, he'd been president for as long as she could remember. Tonight he was talking about the home front. His voice always sounded so smart yet reassuring. It was like he had everything figured out and was letting the country in on it—one person at a time.

Bone didn't always understand what he was saying, like when he was talking about the war of nerves and propaganda. Miss Johnson nodded her head, though, as he spoke. She'd no doubt cover the speech in class tomorrow.

Uncle Junior sat up straight in his chair when the president said folks were fighting in planes over Europe—and deep down in the mines of Pennsylvania. Each of us was playing our part to save democracy, the president explained, and we were going to win.

That made Bone feel good. But she'd never thought about them not winning. Could that happen? America had stepped into the last war to whup the kaiser. In less than a year, Daddy had told her. He'd only seen one battle back then before it was all over. Bone had a bad feeling he'd be gone a lot longer this time.

Then Mr. Roosevelt said there was a manpower problem at home.

"Darn right," Uncle Junior grumbled. He was looking awful tired.

The president said we needed everybody—including women and black folks—to help out where maybe they weren't welcome before. "We can no longer afford to indulge such prejudices . . . ," Mr. Roosevelt said. He also said young and old alike were needed for the war effort at home.

As soon as the broadcast was over, Uncle Ash whistled and Corolla shot out of Bone's lap after her master. They were both out the back door before Bone even could turn around.

"Is Uncle Ash okay?" Bone asked, turning to her grandmother.

"The war talk gets to him sometimes," Mamaw said. "It brings back bad memories. And I think he feels like he can't do his part anymore."

In the last war, Uncle Ash ran off when he was a teenager to join up in Canada—even before America was in the Great War. He spent three years in the trenches and was wounded in action. Some folks said he hadn't been right since.

Uncle Junior stretched his long wiry legs out in front of the fireplace and yawned deeply. "He's served far more than most already. More than I ever could," he added. Uncle Junior had been deemed unfit for duty on account of his flat feet during the last war, and now he was too old. Neither his feet nor his age stopped him from coal mining.

"The war is running on the coal you're mining, son," Mamaw reassured him.

Bone hugged her knees as she sat in front of the fireplace.

Mrs. Price's knitting needles clicked in the silence.

Bone wondered if Mr. Roosevelt had seen Daddy when he visited the army camps.

The clicking stopped. "I hear the powder plant is hiring women." Mrs. Price exchanged a look with Mamaw.

Bone wasn't sure if she meant one of them might go work there. The army had just built a big factory to make ammunition over in Radford. Almost everyone called it the powder plant on account of it making gunpowder and explosives.

"Bone, honey, I stuck some preacher cookies in the icebox for you and Will," Mamaw said. "He should be on his way by now."

Bone knew when she was being got rid of. Plus she was right. Will would be here soon. He'd wanted to listen to the president with his mama. "Yes, ma'am." Bone pulled herself to her feet.

As Bone went into the kitchen, Mamaw answered Mrs. Price, "I'll tell her that."

⮑

The familiar rap on the back door came as Bone opened the icebox.

She slipped on her sweater and joined Will on the back porch, two cool chocolate oatmeal cookies in her hand. The crisp air outside was like the tart taste of green apples. Airish, folks would call it.

Hester Prynne, Miss Johnson's tabby cat, wound her way through Will's legs as he sat on the step. Animals loved silent Will Kincaid. If Uncle Ash were still here, his dogs would be lying at Will's feet, too. Bone pressed a cookie into his hand and plopped down beside him.

She bit into hers. It wasn't as sweet as usual. More oatmeal than cocoa, but still good. She asked him how work was. He knew what she meant. He always did.

He scribbled out something on his little notebook. She'd given it to him—four of them, actually, each with a stub of pencil tied to it—when he started down in the mines.

Beat. Five cars today. Army upped the quota.

"I bet Junior is already snoring away in Daddy's chair," Bone said. Uncle Junior was now Will's boss, the day shift supervisor, since Daddy was off to war. Just for the duration, Junior always added. He'd moved into the boardinghouse just for the duration, too. Bone had a feeling the duration might be longer than she'd thought.

Will wrote something else. *Don't mind. More money.*

Bone nodded. The men got paid per carload. And war needed coal. Loads and loads of coal. For the duration.

He handed her another cocoa-smudged page. *Something odd happened today.*

"Nobody got hurt, did they?" She licked the cocoa off her fingers.

Will shook his head as he wrote. *No, it were during lunch.*

Bone took the slip and watched him as he wrote out a bunch more in his pocket-sized notebook.

I sat down in the cut like usual. Pulled out my pie and biscuits—and this.

He reached into his coat pocket and revealed an empty jelly jar. He set it between them.

She could imagine him sitting on the dirt floor of the mine, his mining light on, spreading out his dinner on a kerchief. Pecan pie. Ham biscuits. Slaw. His mother was a good cook.

You'll never guess what was in it.

"Apple butter." Fall was when everyone churned and canned dark, delicious apple butter. Bone could almost taste it slathered onto a hot biscuit.

Will shook his head.

Edgar Bergen & Charlie McCarthy

Bone stared at the words. They made no sense at all. "What in the Sam Hill are you talking about?" she asked finally. How could a radio show be in a jelly jar?

Will carefully opened the jar just a smidge and held it between them. Sure enough, Bone heard a funny voice say something and then an audience laughed before Will screwed the lid on tight.

"Wait! Was that the dummy?" Bone felt herself going wide-eyed. Charlie McCarthy was Edgar Bergen's ventriloquist dummy. "Do you mean the jar . . ."

Will nodded.

He set the jar back down between them—and inched it toward her.

Bone knew what he wanted. She held her hand over the jar. She could feel warmth radiating off it, like there was an ember or even a coal fire banked down deep inside it. And it was pulling at her. She had a strange feeling, too, one she couldn't put a finger on. This was like nothing she'd ever felt, Gift or not. She snatched her hand away. "I am not touching that thing."

Will put his hand over the jar, protectively. Bone wasn't sure if he was protecting her or it.

"Was that in your daddy's dinner bucket?" She'd gone with Will to get his mining gear at the store. Mr. Scott had saved William Kincaid Sr.'s pail for Will. The bucket had been his granddaddy's, too. And she'd accidently touched it. Bone shivered. She'd seen darkness and black earth and timbers falling on Will's father—before Will snatched the tin bucket out of her hands. That's what his daddy's gear had witnessed in the moments before his death. But this jar was different. It wasn't just a witness. It was something more. And it scared her.

Will was writing something out—on several slips of paper.

"I need to get you a bigger pad," Bone joked uneasily.

He ignored her, handing her the first slip.

Yes, the jar was in Daddy's bucket.

He handed her another slip.

The first time I opened it, I swear I heard his voice.

Bone looked up at Will. He nodded.

"Why didn't you say something then? That was nearly two months ago." Bone was peeved that he'd kept this to himself.

Will shrugged and handed her several slips.

Thought I was hearing things. And the jar hasn't made a peep since then. It's always had something in it. Jam. Pudding. Apple butter. Today, the jar was empty.

Bone allowed how he might think he'd imagined a voice. "Why Bergen and McCarthy?"

He handed her the next slip.

Mama listens to it when she makes my lunch on Sunday.

He let that sink in.

"So you're saying this jelly jar catches sounds?" This was wilder than any story she could think up.

Like lightning bugs in a mason jar.

Will had caught her one of the last lightning bugs of the season. Summer in a jar, she'd thought. She'd put it by her bed, but its light was gone by morning.

"You know that's as crazy as I don't know what."

About as crazy as you reading stories in objects. Will grinned. He'd known exactly what she'd say.

He had her there. Anybody else might call the Reed Gifts crazy. Mamaw could tell with a touch how a plant could be used as medicine. Uncle Ash could feel exactly what was wrong with an animal. And Mama, Bone had learned, could do the same with people—and heal them.

"You want me to read this thing, don't you?"

Will shrugged, but his face said yes. His eyes longed to know.

Bone inched her hand toward the jar again. She could feel its pull. It had a power, a Gift maybe, all its own. Without even touching it, Bone could see little flickers of images. Will Sr. and a very young Will were fishing. The jar was between them, filled with worms. Young Will turned to his daddy and said, "*Knock, knock!*"

Bone snatched her hand away again—and tucked it under her leg.

Will could speak!

She peered at him in the darkness. Bone couldn't recall him ever talking. Some folks said he spoke before his daddy died. Bone was barely walking back then. "Do you remember when you stopped talking?" she asked.

Will stared back at her, his eyes searching her face for a clue. Finally, he shook his head.

"I'm not touching that thing. Not yet anyways."

Will looked away. Bone felt lower than dirt.

"But I got an idea."

His eyes snapped back to her.

"Write down all the things you miss hearing down in the mines. Sunday after church, we'll hunt us up some sounds to put in that jar."

3

THE NEXT MORNING, Ruby walked to school with the Little Jewels. Not that Bone minded. Much. She had the boys in school and Will after supper. She hoped he wouldn't press her again to read that dang jar, at least until they'd had a chance to experiment with it. Mamaw said Bone needed to keep trying out her Gift on ordinary objects—but that jar wasn't ordinary by a long shot. Maybe she just had to see the jar in action for herself. Maybe she ought to talk to Mamaw about it.

The morning dragged on with lessons on the times tables for the fifth graders. Sixth and seventh graders worked on their own math problems. Ruby finished before everyone else and sat staring at the board. Bone's mind kept drifting to the jelly jar as she worked out angles. She finished last.

Then, history got interesting. Miss Johnson's lesson on World War I was interrupted not once but twice by outbursts from Ruby, of all people. She laughed a little too loudly at something Robbie said. And she answered back when Miss Johnson shushed her. Ruby shut her mouth once she had earned chalkboard duty for a week. She'd have to stay after school to clean the boards and erasers in both classrooms—and do whatever else the teachers asked her to do.

Bone suspected Ruby had done it on purpose. She'd thrown Bone a little glance as they all headed out for lunch. She wouldn't be in a hurry to get home to Aunt Mattie neither.

~ ⁊ ~

At the picnic table, Bone slid into her seat under the big sugar maple. She pulled a fried chicken wing (her favorite), two biscuits, and a small jelly jar of apple butter out of her paper sack. The jar was cool to the touch. Bone closed her eyes and concentrated, but she couldn't pick up nary a whiff of story. Not even a hint of Mrs. Price packing it in her lunch. This jar was perfectly ordinary, and maybe even new. Would she have picked up something more if Mama had packed it?

"Bone!" Jake pounded the picnic table with a laugh. "Wake up!"

Bone's eyes shot open. She'd almost forgotten where she was. "Those math problems about put me to sleep," she said.

"Tell us that story about Jack and the mule and the outhouse again," Clay demanded, his mouth already full of ham sandwich. "That's a swell prank." He winked at Jake.

"Yeah but they don't have an outhouse, genius." Jake peeled his hard-boiled egg.

"And we don't have a mule neither." Clay looked wistful. "Remember when Cliff and Carmen took the gates off the cemetery?"

That prank was legendary. The oldest Whitaker brothers took the heavy iron gates off the church cemetery—and swapped them with the wooden gate in front of the parsonage. Aunt Mattie had been hopping mad. Uncle Henry thought it was a hoot. Nobody figured out how Cliff and Carmen did it, and it took five grown men to put the gates back where they belonged.

"Yeah, your brothers were master pranksters," Jake said reverently. "One year they stole about every mailbox on the river road."

Bone remembered that one. When everyone got to school, they found all those mailboxes stacked up inside the johnny house. Bone had been in second grade. Mama had died earlier in the year, and finding the outhouse crammed with mailboxes had made Bone (and everyone else) laugh themselves silly.

"We should really do something," Clay said, looking at Bone. "For them."

"What are you fools talking about?" Bone asked. She had a strong hunch, though, what they wanted.

"We're just talking, mind you." Jake pointed the egg at her as he replied.

"We got to do something on Halloween. A prank. Soaping some windows or throwing some eggs. Something," Clay pleaded.

"And we know it ain't fair to Ruby or the preacher, but . . ." Jake shrugged.

"For Cliff and Carmen," Clay said in a hushed voice. He bowed his head.

"And you." Jake leaned in. "She almost baptized the life right out of you, Bone," he whispered angrily.

"We ain't forgot that," Clay said, looking up.

Bone choked back the taste of iron-cold bathwater and burning anger rising in her throat. She pressed a finger to her lips as Ruby and the Little Jewels appeared right behind the boys.

"The boys are right," Ruby said—not in a whisper. "She deserves a prank, a good one, come Halloween night."

Jake and Clay slid apart to make room for Ruby. Pearl and Opal exchanged worried glances before they sat down beside Bone. She struggled to open the little jelly jar full of apple butter. Mrs. Price had sealed it up tight.

"You know they're talking about Aunt Mattie, right? Your own mother," Bone whispered. She whacked the lid of the jar on the table. The pressure popped, and Bone unscrewed the lid. She was still torn. More than anything, she wanted to plaster Aunt Mattie with rotten eggs. But it didn't seem right on account of Uncle Henry. And Bone couldn't imagine, if she were Ruby, wanting to hurt her own mother like that. Bone would do anything to have her mama back. Still, Aunt Mattie was the reason Mama was gone. She broke open a biscuit.

Ruby ignored her. "What did you have in mind?" she asked the boys. Clay was grinning ear to ear now.

The boys and Ruby quickly settled on egging as both the easiest and most satisfying prank. They could all collect a few eggs over the next two weeks or so without arousing suspicion. Most folks kept some chickens or traded with somebody who did.

"Mamaw has a coop," Ruby said, looking at Bone.

Bone crossed her arms. She still wasn't quite convinced. Nearly. But not quite. Her insides churned like hot apple butter over a fire. Why couldn't they just enjoy Halloween without getting all twisted up about it? Bone took a deep breath, which only cooled off her insides a smidge.

"Come Halloween night, we'll all sneak out about ten o'clock and meet across from the rectory. Right?" Ruby glared at Opal and Pearl until they nodded. Then she picked up her lunch and moved to the next table. The Little Jewels followed.

"Well if that don't beat all," Jake said.

"Who'd'a thunk it?" Clay let out a low whistle.

Bone understood why Ruby was mad at Mattie. Mostly. Aunt Mattie could be awful hard on Ruby. The idea of coating that lily-white rectory in an egg wash of yellow had its appeal, right or not. It would wipe the smug look right off Aunt Mattie's ugly face. Bone slathered a biscuit with apple butter and stuffed it in her mouth.

"She has her reasons," Bone finally said, after about choking on the biscuit. Uncle Henry had a kind word for everyone. "But it still don't make it right." She slapped the lid back on the jar and twisted it shut tight.

Clay looked heartbroken.

"Maybe we can think of a better prank," Bone added. "Something big like what your brothers did."

Clay grinned. Jake slapped the table. "Now you're talking! We need to think bigger!"

"How about another scary story?" Clay asked.

Bone told them about how a young Jack, who was just coming home from the wars, beat three little devils in a poker game and won himself a house.

⌒∽⌒

That evening, the field crickets trilled in the yard, a lingering echo of summer. Bone closed her eyes, listening to their song. She and Will sat on the back porch step, bathed in the warm breeze of an Indian summer night. *All-hallown summer*, Miss Johnson had called it at supper. That was from Shakespeare. It meant a second, brief summer right around Halloween. And it was almost Halloween.

Halloween was great fun, but it was also the dividing line between the lighter and darker halves of the year. Or at least that's what Mamaw said. Summer and fall were warm and bright. Come November, though, everything faded and shriveled up, becoming cool and gray.

Will slid a note across the porch step to her.

Trains, baseball, and your stories.

Those were sounds he missed. Bone sipped her plain ice tea as she read. It was hard to get down at first without the sugar, kind of like the thought of the jelly jar Will held in his lap. "Let's start with something easy."

He unscrewed the lid and held the jar up to her like a microphone. Charlie McCarthy told a joke, and the audience laughed. A child quietly spoke, followed by a man's whisper.

Bone shook her head violently. The jar called to her, but the teensy hairs on her neck bristled and her arm went all gooseflesh and her throat seized up. This jar was nothing to fool with. She wasn't sure they should even touch it, let alone try to catch sounds. She pushed Will's arm away, careful not to touch the jar. Still, she saw a flash of a young Will. The older Will quickly replaced the lid.

"I meant the train," Bone said finally, finding her voice again. "You can't help hearing them around here." Trains rattled along both sides of the river several times a day, stopping to pick up loads of coal at the various mines in the area.

Will nodded. Then he got out his pad and scribbled a question.

Did you see something just now?

Bone took a long drink of tea before she answered. "You were holding the jar as a kid." That's all she'd really seen, but she felt like there was more to it.

Probably helping Mama pack his dinner.

"Uh-huh," Bone replied, not quite convinced that was it. She could swear the young Will had been wearing his Sunday best. The mines never ran on Sunday. She polished off the rest of her tea. "I'll meet you at Flat Woods after church."

Will slurped down the rest of his tea, too, before he left.

Bone remained on the porch steps, waiting to drink in the summery choir of insects again. But the only sound left was Will's boots crunching along the dry ground toward his house.

The crickets were silent.

Summer was truly gone.

Farewell, all-hallown summer.

4

IN SCHOOL THE next day, Bone crossed her arms and glared eyes front as a guest speaker stood before the class. Her belly burned, and she could taste iron. It was Aunt Mattie. Ruby turned her back to talk to Robbie.

"Mrs. Albert is here to tell us about a new scrap drive," Miss Johnson said as she stepped aside.

Aunt Mattie was the queen of scrap drives. She was always holding them at the baseball games. Baseball season was over, though.

Aunt Mattie didn't look in Bone's or Ruby's direction. She was wearing a prim black suit that hung on her bony frame. And she had dark circles under her eyes that no makeup could hide.

Bone uncrossed her arms.

Aunt Mattie cleared her throat. "Eighteen tons of metal goes into one tank." She glanced around the classroom and then checked the piece of paper she clutched in front of her. "And 252 lawn mowers can be turned into an antiaircraft gun."

Bone sat up straight, too. She'd heard Aunt Mattie rattle off these figures before when she collected scrap at the baseball games. But after listening to Mr. Roosevelt talk about the home front, Bone allowed that her aunt might have something important to say.

"The other night the president said that women and kids can help win the war at home. How do we that? Collecting metal! We can turn junk into bullets, guns, tanks, and even ships. Tell your mothers that there's ammunition in their kitchens!" She went on to explain that the Superior Anthracite Company was sponsoring a contest to see which mining community could collect the most scrap. Superior was the company that owned most of the mines in the area. She also went over all the types of metal junk they wanted, from old pots and pans to car parts and metal fences.

Jake poked Bone in the back. "Got another idea for a prank," he whispered.

Bone and Clay both shushed him. Daddy was fixing to go over there, and he could sure use all the tanks or antiaircraft guns he could get. Bone seized upon the idea. She could collect enough scrap to keep Daddy safe.

"All the scrap you gather should be taken over to Centennial Ballpark before November 1," Aunt Mattie concluded. "Oh, and the 4-H Club will also be collecting tin cans. Ruby will be in charge of that."

Ruby popped up to stand beside her mother. "Our club will be going door-to-door on Halloween to collect tin cans. They should be washed and the label removed."

"And flattened," Aunt Mattie added.

Ruby bristled. "And, as I was going to say, flattened. Then we'll take the *flattened* cans over to the ballpark the next day." Ruby walked back to her desk, tightlipped, and didn't even look in Aunt Mattie's direction when she was leaving.

Jake poked Bone in the back again. "Can I tell y'all my idea now?"

Bone turned around.

"What if we get those big iron cemetery gates and put them in the scrap drive?" Jake looked enormously pleased with himself.

"You mean like a prank?" Clay asked. He had a gleam in his eye.

"They would make a good part of a tank," Bone said. She doubted they could budge the gates, let alone get them to the ballpark, but she was game to try. It was better than egging the parsonage. "Maybe we could pull up some of the fencing, at least. It ain't as heavy."

Ruby whirled around in her seat. "We're still egging the parsonage!" she hissed. She looked to Bone for support.

"Well," Bone said. "We might not have time to do both—and the gates are a better prank," she added, looking at Clay.

Ruby turned around in a huff, but Clay was grinning like a Cheshire cat.

"Hot dog!" Jake said.

Bone wasn't sure they could pull off the prank, but the idea of the scrap drive was tugging at her. "Why don't y'all come over Saturday, and let's see what else we can scare up for the scrap drive. We can check out the gates, too." She whispered the last part.

Clay and Jake both nodded their heads vigorously.

Miss Johnson cleared her throat.

Bone turned right around and clamped her mouth shut. She did not want to join Ruby after school. Especially now.

5

IN THE BIG stuffy attic of the boardinghouse, Bone sat staring at the boxes. Downstairs, Mrs. Price was baking pumpkin pies while she listened to the Saturday morning farm report. The scent of cinnamon and nutmeg came up through the floorboards and mixed with the musty smells of the attic. The Phillips boxes only took up a corner under the eaves. Daddy had sold most of the furniture from their old house—except for a few things that were Grandma Eugenia's. An old chest of drawers and a little table Great-granddaddy Oakley made were tucked in between the boxes and the wall. It wasn't a lot. Dust was thick on what little they had.

Bone blew the dust off the first box. Across the top in Daddy's crooked-y handwriting it said, WILLOW'S CLOTHES. Daddy was saving them for Bone, she knew. The box was freshly taped shut. The tape on this box hadn't yellowed like on the others. Mrs. Price had already made a Sunday dress or two for Bone out of Mama's old ones. And this is probably where Daddy had kept the butter-yellow sweater Bone wore now. She was tempted to open the box and run her fingers through the fabric—and the memories. But the yellow sweater already had enough of those, and it doled them out even if she didn't ask for them.

It was almost like Mama was there, watching over her shoulder.

Almost.

Almost was not the real thing.

The attic's pumpkin pie–scented warmth began to press in on Bone. Sweat beaded on her forehead, and she wiped it off on her sleeve.

Bone opened the box marked BONE'S ROOM instead. Inside, she found mostly baby things—like booties—and clothes she'd worn when she was four or five. Bone plucked out a metal rattle. There was also an ugly-as-sin windup metal clown that had scared her as a baby. That could definitely go. She pulled out a small metal horse. In a flash, she could see herself as a tiny tot galloping that horse around the house. Pinto, she'd called it, because once upon a time it was painted that way, with a large splotch of white across its chestnut coat. She had been a cowboy named Bill chasing rustlers who'd taken his cattle.

Bone set Pinto aside. The other things she tossed into the empty box she'd brought with her.

At the bottom of the box filled with baby clothes was a bucket. Bone pulled it out. It was the size of a small mop bucket, but it was white. The sides were painted with blue and purple elephants. Bone didn't remember seeing this at all. She ran a finger over the elephants. They seemed familiar. Closing her eyes, she saw Mama painting them. A storybook was propped up on the table. Bone did remember Mama reading to her from this book. She'd loved the story. Mama was making Bone a sand bucket like the one Ruby had gotten at Virginia Beach. Only hers was small and had a seagull on it. The bucket also came with a tiny red shovel. Bone had wanted one, too, but Daddy said they couldn't afford to go to the beach.

"*It's still an old mop bucket,*" Aunt Mattie had sniffed over Mama's shoulder.

Mama put down the brush. "*You don't think she'll like it?*" She pushed back a long strand of blond hair and wiped her forehead, leaving a streak of blue elephant paint behind.

Aunt Mattie just shrugged. "*Ruby wouldn't.*"

Bone could feel the doubt creeping like cool water into Mama. She kept on painting, though, as Mattie sailed out of the room in her crisp wool suit.

She'd never given the pail to Bone. On account of Aunt Mattie.

Everything bad was on account of Aunt Mattie.

Sweat rolled down Bone's face in earnest now. The attic was getting hotter and hotter, closing in on her. Yet she felt this hollow ache inside.

Bone tossed the bucket toward the attic door. The clatter echoed in the room. She felt a tiny bit better.

"Whoa there, Forever Girl." Uncle Ash poked his head up through the door as the bucket rolled by him. "I see you found some ammunition." He chuckled at his own joke.

"Just some old toys," Bone muttered. It wasn't much to make a tank out of. Then she spotted her tricycle tucked under the table.

"And this," she added as she pulled out the trike. She got a flash of Daddy tightening the bolts and painting it cherry red before he slid it under the Christmas tree. The paint was flaking, and the tires were flat now, but at least she could keep Daddy a little safer with it.

Uncle Ash pulled himself up through the small attic door and stood stooped under the rafter. He put his hand on it to steady himself. "You all right, Bone? Awful lot of memories up here."

"I'm fine," Bone grumbled. She pushed the trike away.

"Uh-huh." Uncle Ash wiped the bead of sweat forming on his brow. "Did I ever tell you about when my Gift started coming on?"

Ash moved to the end of the attic where the big window was. He unbolted it and swung the two halves open like a barn door. A cool breeze rushed in. Bone felt instantly better as the crisp air hit her face. She could breathe again.

"Ever since I was little, it were always my job to feed and generally take care of the dogs, chickens, milk cows, and horses." Uncle Ash stood in the breeze, fanning himself with his hat as he talked. "Daddy always said I was a natural stockman just like his daddy—who, as it turned out, had the same Gift as me. When I was your age, I started getting these flashes whenever I touched an animal. It could get mighty overwhelming in the barn or chicken coop." He put the hat on his head, pushing it back at an angle. Then he reached into his pocket. "So Daddy bought me a pair of these." He tossed some battered old work gloves to Bone.

She slipped them on gratefully. She could tell they were his, but the memories were mostly of him stringing barbed wire or clearing brush, contentedly with a dog or two by his side. She held up her fists to her uncle with a smile. His gloves about swallowed up her hands to her elbow.

He chuckled again. "We can order you some smaller ones from the Sears and Roebuck." Uncle Ash reached out the window and pulled a rope inside. "There's a block and tackle hanging out there." He pointed to a beam mounted above the window. "We can drop the big things out this way." Ash fanned himself with his hat as he looked around. "Lydia said there's an old lawn mower up here we can scrap. And some bed frames." He spotted the rusty reel mower nearby and rolled it over. Then he tied the rope around the lawn mower's handle and lowered it carefully out the window.

"Got it," Clay called up to Uncle Ash.

"I ran into some very eager helpers on the way over," he told Bone.

She helped him wrestle the bed frames to the window. She could see his truck down below already half-full with stuff Jake and Clay had salvaged from their houses. Uncle Ash tied up the frames and lowered them down to the boys.

"Y'all load up the truck," Ash yelled down as he was closing up the window.

"Yessir!" Jake answered.

"Only 251 more lawn mowers to make an antiaircraft gun," Bone said as she boxed up her toys, including the bucket Mama had painted. She'd also found some broken skates, metal cups, and a bent lamp.

"Only nine hundred more tons for a destroyer." Uncle Ash laughed as he wiped his forehead on the sleeve of his flannel shirt.

Bone kicked the tricycle toward the attic door. "Eight hundred and ninety-nine and a half."

"You sure about this, Forever Girl?" Uncle Ash asked as he peered in her box. He called her that after a Cherokee tale they both loved. Forever Boy didn't want to grow up, so he ran off to live with the Little People to be a child forever. The story was a lot like Peter Pan.

Bone nodded. She'd rather Daddy be safe than hang on to childish things.

⁓

Out in the yard, Bone handed her tricycle up to Clay. The truck was only two-thirds of the way full. Not quite enough for an antiaircraft gun yet. Maybe with the cemetery gates and fence they'd have enough—if they could get ahold of them. And maybe they should get other kids to bring in their scrap. Bone pulled off the now sweaty work gloves and tucked them into her belt.

"Why don't y'all go see if the Linkouses or anybody else has got something to throw in?" Bone told the boys. They took off down the road. Pretty soon, Opal and Pearl came by with some old pots and pans. Ruby had a sack of flattened cans she'd already collected. And the boys came back carrying an old wheelbarrow that was missing a wheel.

When Bone reached down to make room for the wheelbarrow, her hand brushed against an old red wagon. She saw the older Whitaker boys, Cliff and Carmen, giving a younger Clay a giant push down the road in the wagon. He held on for dear life as the wagon bumped over the gravel, careening toward an oncoming truck. His big brothers raced after him, yelling at him to steer for the trees. He did and spilled out into grass, laughing, as the truck honked angrily at them all. "Let's do that again," he yelled to his panting brothers. Bone could feel the sheer delight radiating off Clay's wagon.

Bone pulled on the much-too-big gloves again, even though Clay's memory had cheered her up. Except, of course, that Cliff and Carmen were never coming home from the war. The wagon, though, would go toward making sure somebody else's brothers came home. She hoped.

＊ ＊ ＊

As the yellow truck rolled slowly down to the river road, Jake rapped on the cab window. Bone slid it open. She and Corolla were in the front with Uncle Ash while the boys rode in the back, making sure nothing fell out.

"We got room for more junk," Jake said with a wink.

Bone nodded and slid the little window shut. She had promised the boys they could check out the wrought iron gates and fences. "Uncle Ash? How 'bout we stop over by the cemetery and check for junk?" Bone turned to her uncle. "Folks dump stuff over there all the time."

"That's an idea," Uncle Ash said. He put out his cigarette on the side mirror.

Bone wasn't sure if that meant he thought it was a good idea until he turned the truck up the little drive to the graveyard. Clay shot her a not-very-subtle thumbs-up.

Uncle Ash parked the truck at the bottom of the hill near the road. The boys leapt out and made a show of scouring the sides of the road. Bone combed the area near the drive for scrap. People really did throw stuff out here. She picked up a broken car mirror from the grass. She could collect more junk now and size up the cemetery gates later. She wondered if she touched the gates whether she could see how Cliff and Carmen pulled them off. Bone spied a beer can.

Clay yelled, "We'll check up thissa way." The boys sprinted up the gravel drive.

Uncle Ash shook his head as he lit another smoke. "I remember that Halloween the Whitaker boys pinched the front gates," he said. Uncle Ash was no fool.

Corolla raced after the boys.

"Clay has big dreams," Bone said. She picked up the smashed beer can.

They walked up the drive and found the boys standing slack-jawed—next to one of the mine trucks.

Several men were already dismantling the big iron gates and pulling up the picket fence.

One of them was Tiny Sherman. He wiped his brow and walked over to greet Uncle Ash. As always, Mr. Sherman was wearing the Memphis Red Sox cap he'd gotten when he played in the Negro Leagues. He tipped his hat to Bone. Then he explained how the church deacons had hired him and the others to take out the iron gates and fence for the scrap drive.

"It's a bear of a job," Tiny said, wiping his brow with his ball cap.

"I think young Whitaker there was hoping do that himself," Uncle Ash said. "For Halloween."

The men laughed, and Clay turned on his heel and headed back to Uncle Ash's truck.

"Ya'll head back down, too," Ash told Bone and Jake. "I'll be there in a tick."

"Guess we're gonna have to egg the parsonage after all," Jake whispered to Bone as they walked away.

Bone groaned. *Maybe they would.*

6

INSIDE THE CHURCH was as warm as a summer's day, and the deacon droned on, reading chapter and verse. At least Uncle Henry's sermons had kept Bone awake. Mostly. Her eyelids slid shut. She was floating in the river under a clear blue sky and a butter-yellow sun—until Mrs. Price's elbow brought her back to the here and now. She nodded toward Mattie and Ruby, seated in their usual spot near the front of the church. Ruby was whispering angrily to her mother.

". . . and Reverend Sullivan and his family will be arriving in January," the deacon spoke loudly to drown out Ruby.

A hymnal slammed against a pew. Ruby stormed down the aisle. Aunt Mattie quietly steamed after her, her head hung low but determined. The outer door slammed shut.

"What was that about?" Bone whispered to Mrs. Price.

"The new preacher."

"Uh-oh." Bone hadn't thought about the church replacing Uncle Henry, at least so soon.

"How dare you act that way in church!" Aunt Mattie's voice carried straight through the walls.

"You knew! It's your fault!" Ruby screeched back. "It's all your fault!"

The deacon called for hymn 145, but "What a Friend We Have in Jesus" didn't quite drown out the fight raging outside.

When church let out, Ruby and Mattie were still going at it.

⁀᷄᷇᷄

Bone ran up the back steps of the boardinghouse and changed into her dungarees and sweater. It wanted to show her something, but she brushed the memory aside. She was getting better at ignoring the stories some objects held—familiar ones, at least, like her mama's sweater. As Bone clomped back down the steps, a voice called from the kitchen. "Whoa there, Forever Girl!" Uncle Ash, Junior, and Mamaw were drinking coffee over a plate of ham biscuits and greens. A bouquet of wildflowers lay between them. "Where's the fire?" Uncle Ash asked.

"Meeting Will." Bone paused to scoop up a couple of biscuits from Mamaw's outstretched plate. They smelled warm and buttery, and Bone's stomach grumbled. She bit into one. The ham was salty and bursting with flavor. She chewed for a moment before she remembered the fight. "Well, the fire was at church. You should've seen Ruby and Aunt Mattie go at it."

Mamaw let out a long sigh and then gulped down her coffee. "I better get over there before they scratch each other's eyes out."

Bone started to leave. "Hold your horses, missy," Mamaw said as she stood and rinsed out her coffee cup. Then she tore off some wax paper, wrapped up two more ham biscuits along with the one Bone hadn't yet bitten into, and handed them to Bone. "Will's gonna want more than one biscuit." She kissed Bone on the forehead and vanished out the door before Bone could even thank her. Acacia Reed did not dillydally.

"What were they fighting about?" Ash asked as he passed his brother another biscuit.

Bone shrugged. "They were outside for most of it, but whatever it was, they were loud." Bone thought for a second. "Ruby ran out of the service. She yelled something about it all being Mattie's fault."

"What was her fault?" Ash asked, sipping his coffee.

Bone chewed the last bite of the salty, buttery goodness before she answered.

"The new preacher, I guess. The deacon announced that a reverend somebody would be coming in January."

Bone's uncles exchanged a look. "I was afraid of that," Junior finally said. "The church can't go on without a minister for too long."

And the new preacher would live at the parsonage, Bone realized. "Where will they go?" she asked. Aunt Mattie didn't work for the church or the mines. In fact, she didn't work. Paid work, at least. Could they stay in Big Vein? Bone didn't want Ruby to leave. No wonder she's mad!

"We'll figure out something—if she'll let us help." Uncle Junior poured himself another cup of coffee.

"You go meet Will." Uncle Ash lit a Lucky Strike. He tossed a piece of ham to Corolla.

❧

Will was waiting for her by the entrance to Flat Woods—with that jar in his hands. "You are carrying that thing," she told him as she marched right by.

The trees were alight with burnt oranges and reds, and leaves fluttered to the ground around them as they walked. The woods were quiet except for the distant barking of dogs. On a Sunday, Mr. Childress liked to run his dogs in the hills up by the mines. She and Will stayed to the flats, down by the river. Tracks wound along either side of the river, and a train was due through any time now.

They walked along the well-worn path to Picnic Rock. At least that's what Bone called it. It was just a flat, half-buried boulder on the edge of the woods. You could sit and watch the river and the trains go by. Will spread out his jacket on top of the rock, and Bone unwrapped the ham biscuits.

As they ate, Bone told Will about the carnival being canceled and what the boys and Ruby wanted to do.

Will shook his head over that. Wiping his fingers on his trousers, he got out his pad and pencil. *That won't end well.*

Bone nodded. "But Ruby is so angry with her mother. You should've heard them going at it in church!"

What was the fight about?

"The new preacher." She told Will what she'd told her uncles.

Will held up his first note again. *That won't end well.*

Bone laughed, but it was probably too true.

Dogs barked as they bounded through the upper woods. A train rattled by on the opposite side of the river. But Will didn't move. Bone figured he was waiting for the 1:15 to come along this side. The baying of the hounds got closer and closer.

"Mr. Childress must be working his dogs this afternoon," Bone finally said. He liked to say he was a whole lot nearer to the Almighty out in the mountains than he was in church. The dogs sounded like they were chasing something this way. "You don't hear that down in the mines." Bone cocked her head toward the dogs. Will nodded but kept the lid on the jar.

A few minutes later, the Virginian blew its whistle as it came around the bend. Will unscrewed the metal lid, stood up on the rock, and held the jelly jar toward the sound, like he was waiting for it to fly in. Bone pictured him catching that lightning bug for her at the end of summer. It seemed like a lifetime ago.

As the whistle died out and the train's brakes squealed along the rails, Will screwed the lid back on tight. The silence in the woods was almost deafening. Then Bone heard the trampling of leaves behind them as three hounds bounded toward them. They headed straight for Will. He hopped down from the rock to greet them.

"Heel," a voice called. The pack broke off and returned to their owner.

"Hey, Mr. Childress," Bone said as the older gentleman looked over his dogs. "How's the hunting?"

"Terrible," he said, straightening up. "Only caught me a pair of skinny sweethearts." Mr. Childress grinned.

Will blushed. Bone might have done so if anybody else had called them that. Mr. Childress liked to tease everybody. It was just his way.

"Come on, girls." He motioned the dogs forward, and they bounded silently toward the river road.

Moments later, Mr. Childress's voice echoed through the woods as he talked to someone up by the road.

"Maybe we should test your theory somewhere quieter," Bone said.

Will motioned for Bone to follow him, and he took off at a brisk pace up the hill past the mines and back down again. Though it was just past midday, the woods were darker here. At night, some folks had seen ghost lights bobbing through the trees. Mamaw said it was probably just the eyes of animals or foxfire, a fungus that glowed. But Bone couldn't help thinking of Jack wandering the world with his lantern—and of the nightmare she kept having about Daddy. He was lost in a dark, strange forest, feeling his way from tree to tree. Sometimes the trees were bodies.

All of a sudden, she and Will emerged out of the woods. And there was the cemetery. It was on a slope like just about everything in Big Vein.

"Maybe this is a bit too quiet," Bone mumbled as she followed Will into the graveyard. *And full of bodies.* Bone could see where Tiny and his crew had pulled up the fence that had surrounded the cemetery. A stone path wound through its middle. The path led down to the gates, or where they had once stood. Will stopped at a little stone bench in the center of the path. He opened the jar just a crack, and they both leaned in. The blast of the train whistle pushed them back as it exploded out of the jar. Dogs barked after it—followed by crickets, Charlie McCarthy's voice, and the tinkle of laughter. Will clapped the lid on tight before anything else could get out.

He leapt up, holding the jar tight. *See!* his face said. He held the jar out to her.

"Well, I'll be jiggered!" Bone said. All the sounds were there.

A thousand things raced through her mind. How could this object get the power to do that? It caught sounds and kept them. Charlie McCarthy was still there. The sounds could fly out, but something pulled them back in, like moths to a porch light.

Bone heard a crunch of boots on the path. Will turned quickly to the grave nearest the bench and put the jar by the headstone. Then Corolla was at Bone's feet.

"Forever Girl, Will, what are y'all doing up here?" Uncle Ash shifted the bouquet of wildflowers from one hand to the other so he could shake Will's hand just like he always did.

Will nodded his head toward the gravestone. "Ah," Uncle Ash replied. "Say hey to your daddy for me. He was a good man. Fought in the Ardennes, I think."

Bone peered past Will and read the gravestone for the first time.

WILLIAM A. KINCAID SR.
B. MAY 5, 1900 D. NOVEMBER 1, 1932

Will had brought her to his daddy's grave to listen to the jelly jar. He turned back to the headstone.

Uncle Ash laid a hand on her shoulder. "Let's let Will have a minute alone with his father." He motioned for her to follow him and Corolla. Picking his way carefully through two rows of folks, Alberts and Scotts mostly, he paused at a grave where the dirt was not yet covered with grass.

HENRY FRANCIS ALBERT
B. JANUARY 7, 1905 D. OCTOBER 7, 1942

Ruby's father.

Uncle Ash dug something out of his pocket and placed it on the base of the grave marker. The thing was a small reddish-brown cross-shaped rock. A fairy stone. Bone had heard about these but never seen one. They were supposed to ward off evil.

"We took Henry over to Fairy Stone Lake for his stag do," Ash said with a grin. "Before him and Mattie got hitched." The area around the lake was one of the only places in the world where fairy stones could be found. The Cherokee legend was that the Little People wept when they heard Christ died. Their tears formed tiny crosses when they hit the ground.

Then Ash headed to the last row. Trees grew just beyond the grave markers. One was a weeping willow, dripping with gold leaves. Another was a scraggly gray tree that was already bare. It was a hawthorne, Bone realized.

Kiawah and Kitty Hawk, her uncle's hounds, were already there, flanking either side of one grave. Corolla raced to greet them.

WILLOW REED PHILLIPS
B. JANUARY 6, 1901 D. MARCH 16, 1936

Mama.

Bone hadn't visited her grave as long as she could remember. Daddy didn't go. Not even on Decoration Day, when the whole community spruced up the cemetery.

Uncle Ash laid the flowers across her grave.

Bone shifted from foot to foot, unsure what to do. She watched her uncle neaten up the grave, tossing the old dried-up flowers off into the woods. The dogs stretched out in the cool green grass behind the headstones.

"Daddy says she's not there," Bone finally managed to say. The tree bearing her name rustled in the breeze. Uncle Ash didn't seem to notice.

"Nope, she ain't," he said. "But graveyards—like funerals— are more for the living than the dead." He struck a light off a neighboring headstone and lit his Lucky Strike. The stone said, HAWTHORNE REED SR. Papaw. Between him and Mama was a small plaque in the ground that read ELDER HAWTHORNE. He'd been barely born when he died.

Bone had seen Papaw whittling the wood and dreaming of baby Elder when she'd touched a toy truck he'd made.

"Gives you a quiet place to come and think about folks you've lost and such. Sometimes you just need to talk." Uncle Ash took a long drag off his cigarette.

Bone didn't need a separate place to think about Mama, especially with the yellow sweater always nudging her along. Like now. Running her finger over the sleeve, she could see Mama coming to lay wildflowers on Papaw's grave. She plucked out one lone flower and placed it on Elder's grave with a kiss. Mama's sorrow was like a deep river current pulling her under. Bone plunged her hands into her dungaree pockets to avoid touching the sweater—or anything around her.

She told Uncle Ash what she'd seen. "Why did she put a flower on Elder's grave? She never knew him."

Uncle Ash ran his fingers through his hair before answering. "She lost a child before you, honey. It never made it to getting born, though. So she'd talk to Elder, at least until you came along."

Bone had always wanted a brother or sister, but Daddy had never talked about it. He was good at not talking about things.

"What do you talk to Mama about?" Bone asked.

He motioned for both of them to sit down next to the grave. Bone felt funny doing that, but she picked a spot between Elder and Mama.

Uncle Ash sank down to the grass with his back against the side of Papaw's headstone. "Well, lately, I been talking to her about how to help you with your Gift," he said. "Like she'd done me."

He'd told her about this before. Mama helped him figure out how to really use his Gift, even after he got home from the war. But he hadn't been real specific.

"How exactly did she do that?" Bone could feel the cool earth creeping up into her bones. She hesitated before she wrapped the sweater around her. This time, she caught a flash of Mama holding a baby, holding her. This time joy flowed through Mama, with just an undercurrent of sadness. Sometimes she couldn't brush aside what the sweater wanted to show her—nor did she want to. Bone buttoned it up to her throat.

"When I was a boy, not too much older than you, Willow talked old Doc Smith, the vet from Radford, into letting me work for him. It was mostly shoveling manure and holding down calves for shots. But Willow told me to practice on animals he'd already diagnosed."

Bone had seen her uncle's Gift in action many times. He could lay his hand on a dog or horse and see exactly what ailed it. "How did that help?"

"I could see what was going on inside the animal, but I didn't know what it all meant. Couldn't tell a gallbladder from a hole in the ground. And sometimes I'd get lost in all those innards, especially if a couple things were wrong. So if the doc said the horse had the strangles, I knew to focus on the windpipe. I learned what that kind of infection looked like." Uncle Ash thankfully did not describe in detail exactly what equine distemper did to a poor horse's insides. The strangles was a pretty darn descriptive name anyways.

"Willow done the same thing with the traveling nurse, helping her with her rounds and such. And Mother had Grandma Daisy to teach her. She didn't have the Gift, but she knew everything about herbs."

Mamaw could touch a plant and see exactly what it could do in the body. Great-grandma Daisy could tell her what something meant, like chamomile tea being good for colic. So could her books. Mama, Ash, and Mamaw each had someone like that to help them figure out what they were seeing—and what to do with it.

"But neither me nor Mother can figure out how we might could help you with your Gift."

Bone nodded. Her Gift wasn't quite the same as theirs. She didn't need a book to tell her what was happening when that deer got shot with the arrowhead or when Tiny Sherman got beat by those white men. "I know what I'm seeing, most of the time, leastways." Mamaw had tried to help Bone by giving her Papaw's baseball cap. It had good memories in it, and she really didn't mind seeing those. Other things—like people getting hurt and dying—she did mind seeing. A lot.

"What can I help you with, Bone?" Uncle Ash took her hand in his.

Bone could see in his eyes how much he wanted, even needed, to help her like Mama had helped him. The real problem was that Bone didn't know what good her Gift was.

"My Gift is useless!" Bone blurted out. "What am I supposed to do with it?"

Uncle Ash sat back. One of the hounds raised his head and looked at her through sleepy eyes for a moment, before letting it thunk back onto the grass.

"Sorry, Kiawah," Bone murmured to the dog.

Uncle Ash lit another Lucky before saying anything. "Forever Girl, I do not know the answer to that very important question.

I didn't have to think hard about what to do with my Gift. Neither did Mama or Willow or even Junior." He took a long drag on his cigarette and let out a lopsided smoke ring. "Perhaps the more you work with your Gift, and open yourself up to it, the more obvious it'll be what the Gift wants you to do."

"What *it* wants me to do?" Bone asked. She wasn't sure she liked this answer one bit.

"I'm not sure how to explain this." Uncle Ash took another puff and ran his fingers through his hair. "When I touch an animal, I try to be real quiet and ask—in my mind—what the body is trying to tell me. And my Gift leads me to what's wrong. But I got to be ready to do it—and respectful of the animal and my Gift, too. Does that make sense?"

Bone nodded. "Like I did with Mama's sweater." When she finally decided to read her mother's sweater to find out what really happened, Bone asked it to reveal its secrets. And she had to be ready to hear them. Hugging the sweater now, she caught flashes of many memories. There was a lot of happy and sad in this ordinary pile of yarn. "What if there's a lot of things wrong with an animal? Does asking help you find the most important one?"

"I suppose so. Like I said, it's easy to get lost in your Gift." He stubbed the cigarette out on his boot and put the remains in his shirt pocket. "Do you see a lot of things happening all at once in an object?"

"Sometimes," Bone replied. The sweater kept sending her memories from any old time in her mama's life. "It's hard to tell the *when* or order of things."

"Maybe we work on that." Uncle Ash lit yet another Lucky Strike. "Willow would know exactly what to do. She was smart that way." He leaned back against Papaw's tombstone and breathed out three perfect smoke rings.

"But she's not here," Bone said quietly. She knew why, thanks to her Gift. She'd died saving Aunt Mattie, of all people. A shard of coal burned in her gut. Maybe egging the rectory wasn't such a bad idea after all. Bone saw a flash. Mama was whispering something to Aunt Mattie as she slept. Bone jerked away her hands and wrapped her arms around her knees to avoid touching the butter-yellow sweater. Uncle Ash raised an eyebrow at her but didn't say anything.

They sat for a long moment in the grass, listening to their own thoughts. Bone tried to imagine if Mama were still here. Would she and Bone cook together like Aunt Mattie and Ruby? Would they read together? Would Bone ride along with Mama on her calls? Bone fingered her sleeve, and the sweater showed her a four-year-old Bone toddling after Mama, trying to carry her nursing bag up the stairs. She remembered that, vaguely. But what about now? Would she and Mama listen to the radio and plot the course of the war together on her *National Geographic* map? Would Daddy have even gone if Mama were still here? Bone doubted it.

Wait, is the sweater following my thoughts? Is that why it prods me with memories from time to time?

A train whistle blew, jolting Bone back to the here and now. And Will and the jelly jar. She glanced over to see if he was still with his daddy. He was—and he was screwing the lid back on.

"Uncle Ash?" Bone hugged her knees tight.

"Hmm?"

"You ever hear of an object that had a Gift of its own?"

Uncle Ash stubbed out his Lucky Strike on his boot. "What do you mean?"

"It can do something, maybe has a special power. Like the sack in that story Soldier Jack." In it, Jack does a kindness for an old man, who then gives him a sack with the power to catch anything.

"'Wickety-whack, get in my sack?'" Uncle Ash raised an eyebrow again as he said this. It was part of the story. It was what Jack had to say to trap something in the sack. He captured a turkey, a couple of robbers, and even Death himself in that bag.

Bone nodded. "But with a real object."

"Like what?" Uncle Ash sat up straighter.

"A jar." She glanced in Will's direction again. He was gone.

Uncle Ash followed her gaze and nodded. Then he thought on it as he lit another cigarette and took a long drag. "Well, when I was in France, I heard of relics that folks thought could heal. Holy objects. But I always thought that was more on the believer than the object. Folks want to believe things." He took another

72

puff. "I also heard of stories—just stories, mind you—of haunted objects. Like that mirror over in Radford at the Ingles House. A lady haunts it. But that's just a campfire story."

"I like them if they ain't true." Bone shivered. It was getting a bit airish out. "What did the mirror do?" She leaned in, unable to resist a good story.

Uncle Ash smiled as he pulled himself to his feet. He reached a hand down to Bone. "Come on, dogs," he commanded, and they sprung up and raced ahead of him. "I'll tell you on the way to the truck." They stepped their way gingerly back to the path and down toward the front gates, Ash talking as they walked. "Well, some folks say this woman was passing by the mirror when a lightning bolt struck right outside. The flash seared her image into the silver—kindly like a photograph. When she died years later, her ghost was seen in the mirror. Now I've been to that house, and I didn't see anything in that mirror—other than my own ugly mug."

Still, that was definitely an object Bone did not want to touch.

They walked through what was left of the cemetery gates. The men had left the stone pillars behind. The graveyard looked exposed and naked without the big iron gates. Bone marveled again at the thought of the Whitaker brothers getting them off their hinges and carting them away. The pale yellow pickup truck was parked in the patch of gravel down below. The dogs wrestled in the grass nearby.

Bone rested her hand on the warm hood of the battered old truck. She'd touched it a thousand times before, but this time she saw a long stretch of beach unfolding in front of her. Uncle Ash was at the wheel, the dogs hanging their heads out the windows. The air tasted crisp and salty. The low murmur of a Christmas carol played on the radio. She felt a happy, peaceful feeling, like she was free and nothing hung over her, like she could breathe.

Uncle Ash eyed her as she stood, hand on the truck.

"So that's where you go before Christmas!" Bone couldn't help grinning.

He laughed and whistled for the dogs—all named after beaches in the Carolinas—to clamber into the back of the truck. Kiawah and Kitty Hawk leapt into the rusting bed. Corolla hopped up into the cab.

"Let that be our little secret, Bone." Uncle Ash stopped, his hand on the open door, and looked at Bone peculiarly. "But that does give me an idea." He motioned for her to slide in.

When she did, Corolla plopped his butt in her lap. Bone hugged the little dog. He smelled like Ivory soap and biscuits and fallen leaves.

Uncle Ash took one last look at the graveyard before getting in. "Thank you, Sis. Why didn't I think of that?" He checked the mirror before backing the truck out of the cemetery.

This time Bone raised an eyebrow at him.

BONE SWIRLED HER oatmeal around with a spoon, in no real hurry to get to school. She was thinking about people's secrets—Will's, Uncle Ash's, Mama's—when Uncle Ash slid the letter in front of her.

"Maybe this'll perk up your appetite," he said. "Just picked it up at the store." The Scott Brothers' store also served as the post office. Uncle Ash handed Mrs. Price the rest of the mail, and poured himself a cup of coffee.

The postmark said Ft. Benning, Georgia, and the handwriting was Daddy's. Bone tore the envelope open.

Dear Bone,

You might not hear from me for a few weeks. Don't worry none, though. We're just on the move. Can't say where I am

or where we're going. Just wanted to tell you how much I
love you. A bushel and a peck, as my mother used to say.
I hope Junior, Ash, and Mamaw are looking out for you.
I'm awful sorry about putting you with Mattie. I blame
myself. Grief can make a body do crazy things. Don't be
angry with her.

Love,
Daddy

Bone wasn't sure if Daddy meant him or Mattie doing the crazy things. Maybe he meant both. After Mama died, he threw their mattress down the steps at their old house—and slept on the floor in Bone's room for days. She'd wake up sometimes when he'd lay a hand on her forehead in the middle of the night. *Just see if you're warm*, he'd say. Bone realized now what he was doing. He was scared she might get the influenza, too.

"Why the frown, Forever Girl?" Uncle Ash sat down with a black cup of coffee.

"Daddy says they're moving out but he can't say where." She showed Uncle Ash the letter.

"Loose lips—" Uncle Ash started to say but quickly took an extra-long drink of coffee. "I mean he's got to be careful. Might be Nazi spies steaming open our mail."

Uncle Ash was trying to make her laugh, but Bone had seen the posters, too, hanging down at the Scott Brothers' store.

Loose Lips Might Sink Ships. A boat was going under amid a cloud of black smoke. Just like Uncle Henry's ship had. Just like Daddy's might.

"So what are you all planning for Halloween?" Uncle Ash asked. "Got a costume for the carnival yet?"

"Didn't you hear?" Mrs. Price topped off his coffee. "The carnival's been canceled."

Bone pushed away from the table, tucking the letter into her schoolbooks. "I'd better get to school."

"Mattie?" She heard Uncle Ash ask Mrs. Price as she headed out the door.

Bone took off running toward school, not even waiting for Ruby. The leaves crunched under her feet. What would she do if something happened to Daddy? She shoved down a thought. If Mama were here, she wouldn't have to worry. Daddy probably wouldn't have even left. She wouldn't have let him.

Mattie. Some folks said Uncle Henry joined up on account of Aunt Mattie. She drove him away with her with her spiteful ways. Bone could understand why Ruby blamed her mother for everything.

Bone fumed over this throughout math, geography, and history.

❧

At lunch, Jake and Clay slipped into the bench beside Bone, flanking her. Jake rolled two hard-boiled eggs out onto the picnic table, cracking their shells. He passed Clay one. They both started peeling theirs methodically.

"I sure hate to waste a good egg," Jake said, picking off a piece of shell.

"I know, but it'd be for a good cause." Clay flicked a shard into the grass.

Bone held up her hand. She could see what they were doing. A blind man would. "I do not want to hear about egging the parsonage." The boys were pushing it. And Bone hated being wheedled into doing something—even if she was coming around to their cause. She wasn't quite there yet.

The boys shut up but kept peeling their eggs.

Bone unwrapped her sandwich. Peeking under the slice of white bread, she crinkled up her nose. Spam. She took a tentative bite. The meat was an odd mix of salty and mushy. Not terrible, but not country ham or fried bologna.

Jake shoved the entire egg in his mouth, almost gagging himself.

Bone tried hard not to giggle. She failed. The boys were deviling her into a better mood.

"We could use soap," Clay said as he admired his own cleanly picked egg.

"No, definitely eggs," Ruby said as she sat down. "Rotten ones."

"Yup, eggs," Jake said, about choking on his again until Bone slapped him on the back. He spit pieces of yolk across the picnic table.

Bone looked away, suddenly glad for the canned lunch meat in front of her. She might not ever eat another hard-boiled egg again. "You know what they're talking about, right?" Bone asked her cousin.

"The whole seventh grade does. Probably the whole school does. And I'm still in. Are you?" The glint of anger almost twinkled in Ruby's eyes. "If you're my friend, you'll do this, too." She said it in a quiet, flat voice that sounded exactly like her mother's.

Bone narrowed her eyes at Ruby. The fury boiling up inside her choked off her words. She wanted to say that she wasn't one of the Jewels to be bullied into doing whatever Ruby wanted. The words stuck in her craw. Bone had been that close to saying yes before Ruby opened her big mouth. Now Bone just wanted to wipe the ugly clean off her cousin's face.

"Now you done it," Clay whispered, shaking his head.

Bone methodically wrapped the remains of her Spam sandwich in the wax paper, put it back in the paper sack, and pushed herself up. She was fixing to go eat her lunch inside. Alone.

"She didn't mean that," Jake told Bone. "Did you?" he implored Ruby.

Ruby glowered at Bone. Then she took a deep breath. "Wait," she said quietly. "I didn't mean to say it that way."

Bone found her voice. "The acorn doesn't fall far from the tree," she told Ruby. Bone kept standing. The boys stifled a gasp.

It took a moment for the penny to drop. When it did, Ruby rose in a very Mattie-like huff. She motioned for the Little Jewels to follow. They hesitated. Ruby took another deep breath and smoothed out her dress. "Please think about it," she said cool as a cucumber. Ruby gathered up her lunch and went to another table. Pearl and Opal exchanged a worried look and followed.

Bone sunk back down into her seat.

Jake shook his head ruefully. "Aw, forget her."

"She's just grieving," Clay said. "She can't help it." He tucked into his egg without much relish. He set it down. Jake put a hand on his friend's back.

Clay's whole family was grieving.

Bone spread out her lunch again. She stared at the half-eaten sandwich for a moment and then pushed it aside. Clay's head was bowed over the remains of his egg. "Uncle Ash told me this story the other day."

Clay looked up with a grin.

"There's this haunted mirror . . ."

8

ALL WILL WANTED to talk about was the dad-blame jar.

Will you read it?

Can we do another experiment?

Will you read it if we try all the things on my list?

Bone wasn't ready by a long shot to touch the jar. (And she was still mad at Ruby.) Plus she wasn't sure capturing more sounds would get them any closer to solving its mystery. They needed to know more about what had happened to Will's father in order to figure out what was going on with the jar. She'd seen just a teeny bit of his death when she'd touched the dinner bucket. As soon as she'd laid her fingers on the metal, it all went dark inside her head. She could hear the moaning of timbers giving way and the rumble of rock collapsing around her. That was scary enough. The jar somehow had a power of its own, one that pulled at her and captured sounds. What had happened down in that mine to cause that?

"I think we need to do a little detective work first," she told Will. He was none too happy about it, but he gave in. And the logical person to start with was the one who'd given him the jar in the first place, the only other person who'd been right there when Mr. Kincaid died. "Meet me at the store after work tomorrow," she told Will.

∼

The war had changed the Scott Brothers' store in small ways. It still had almost everything a miner or his family needed. The older men still played checkers over a cracker barrel. Only now, war posters plastered the walls. LOOSE LIPS MIGHT SINK SHIPS. SAVE GAS BY SHARING CARS. JOIN THE ARMY. TOGETHER WE CAN DO IT. GET IN THE SCRAP! THEIR LIVES ARE IN YOUR HANDS! THERE'S AMMUNITION IN YOUR KITCHEN! Some of the shelves were barer. And you had to buy some things—like sugar—with a war ration book.

Bone patted her pocket to make sure hers was still there. Both Mamaw and Mrs. Price had stressed the importance of keeping track of it. In fact, Mrs. Price usually kept it for Bone, but today she'd had to run over to Radford. She'd entrusted Bone with getting the boardinghouse some sugar for canning. Bone waited for Will to get off work so they could kill two birds with one stone, so to speak. Will had to talk to Mr. Scott about that jar.

Mrs. Linkous was ahead of them in line. Bone watched as she opened up her and the twins' ration books and tore off the little numbered squares. Bone got hers out. The small paper book was about the size of a postcard. Across the front it said, UNITED STATES OF AMERICA WAR RATION BOOK ONE. Bone opened it. Inside, her name, address, height, weight, eye and hair colors, and age were filled in. Some of the numbered squares were gone already. Mrs. Price usually did the shopping for the entire boardinghouse. How did she know which ones to use? The book didn't say what number was for what rationed thing.

"What can I get you, Bone?" Mr. Scott asked.

"Mrs. Price wants some sugar for canning and some coffee." Bone laid out the open ration book on the counter. "Which one do I use?" she asked.

Mr. Scott pointed at numbers 15 and 19 before grabbing the bags from under the counter. Bone tore off the little pieces of paper, careful not to rip the other numbers, and handed the squares to Mr. Scott. He slid five pounds of sugar and one pound of coffee across the counter in exchange.

"Thanks, Mr. Scott."

"That radio hasn't come in yet, Will," Mr. Scott said as he wiped down the counter. "Everything is a mite slower on account of the war."

Bone turned to Will. He'd neglected to mention he'd ordered a new radio. "Did y'all's break?" she asked.

Will nodded as he tucked the sack of sugar under his arm. He didn't look her in the eye.

An idea began to form at the back of Bone's brain—but they were there to learn about something else. Bone turned again to Mr. Scott. "Will and me want to talk to you about something, if you have the time." Bone took the lead, just as she had when they'd ordered Will's mining gear.

Mr. Scott stopped wiping. "Of course, what about?" he asked, amused.

Bone leaned in to whisper it, but Will slid a note across the counter.

Could you tell me about that day?

Mr. Scott went white, but he nodded. "Tell you what, I'll meet you on the porch after I take care of these ladies. Help yourself to a cold drink."

Mrs. McCoy and her daughter had come in behind them, war ration books in hand.

Will slid a dime across the counter and tucked the pound of coffee under his arm with the sugar. Bone pulled a Nehi and an RC Cola out of the cooler in the corner. Over it hung a poster for a special exhibition baseball game in Pulaski. The semipro team was raising money for war bonds. "Will, over here!" Bone called. "I found you some baseball." It was on his list of things he missed down in the mines. She handed him his pop.

Will grinned as he gulped down his RC Cola.

The game was Sunday. The poster said to bring tin cans if you couldn't afford the fifty-cent admission. Bone was sure she could talk Uncle Ash into driving them.

Outside on the porch, Bone settled down in one of the rockers to enjoy her grape soda. The thing about the radio niggled at her, though. She watched Will. He set down the sugar and coffee sacks on the porch railing and commenced to pace back and forth, his boots practically wearing a groove in the wood planks.

"When did the radio break?" Bone asked, taking a sip of soda. She had an uneasy feeling she knew the answer.

Will stopped in his tracks and just stood there looking out over the slag pile.

"Was it after you heard Charlie McCarthy come out of that darn jar?" It did more than record sounds. It broke the radio somehow, like lightning maybe, shorting out its insides.

Will's shoulders sagged a bit as he nodded.

He knew—and he hadn't told her.

What if she'd touched that darn thing? What if she'd told it a story? Would it have shorted her out, too? Bone gripped the Nehi bottle, fighting the urge to hurl it at the back of Will's stubborn, fat head.

Lucky for Will, the screen door swung open. Bone took a deep breath—and a long drink of her Nehi. It didn't quite cool her insides off.

Mr. Scott limped out and eased himself into the chair beside Bone. He waved Will to sit down, but he just leaned against the banister, one hand in his jacket pocket.

"I was wondering when you were going to ask me about it, son." Mr. Scott looked up at Will. The older man took a moment or two to collect his thoughts. "It was a day like any other. William and me were taking timbers out of one of the old shafts." He explained how back then they were digging so fast the mill couldn't keep up with timbers, so they often took them out of closed-down shafts and reused the wood in new ones.

Will nodded. He'd told Bone they still do this, only now it was because they didn't have enough people to work the mill.

"All my brothers—except the youngest—were down in the mines back then," he said wistfully. Mr. Scott had four brothers, and none of them mined anymore. The youngest played semipro ball but had just signed up for the Army Air Corps.

"It was lunchtime, and we were sitting in the shaft where we'd been working. We were talking about football—and our boys. He was going to take you to the college game that Saturday. He wanted to show you around campus—even if you was only five. He had dreams for you, young man."

Will shifted uneasily. Then he pulled up a milk crate and sat down, looking up at Mr. Scott.

"Suddenly it all went to hell in a handbasket. I don't remember much of anything after that, not until I woke up in the hospital in Radford with a crushed leg." Mr. Scott rubbed his left knee. "I cried like a little baby when they told me William didn't make it out alive." He paused for a long moment. Then he pushed himself to his feet and shook out his bad leg. "Can't sit too long or it gets to hurting me."

Will got up, too.

"William and me were like Bone's daddy and Junior," Mr. Scott told Will. "We were always working together—and we were good friends. What makes me the saddest is him not seeing what a fine young man you turned out to be, Will." He held out his hand.

Will shook Mr. Scott's hand and then headed down the road, his hand in his jacket pocket again.

Bone started after him but thought better of it. He needed some time to himself, and she still needed to ask Mr. Scott something. "How did you get the dinner bucket?"

"Junior brought it to me. After the funeral, I think." Mr. Scott watched Will walking away. "William really wanted Will to go to college. Or maybe join up and see the world. There's nothing wrong with mining, mind you, but William wanted so much more for his son. I want more for my kids." Mr. Scott's youngest son had just signed up for the marines. He turned to limp back into the store. Stopping in the doorway, he added, "Right now, I'm just praying they make it out of this war alive."

Bone watched Will walk past his house and down the road toward the river, one hand still in his pocket. Was he going to the cemetery again? Was that jelly jar in his pocket?

9

AFTER SUPPER, BONE spread her homework—and the new *National Geographic*—out on the kitchen table. Miss Johnson gave Bone the magazines after she was done reading them. This one had a pull-out map of South America that Miss Johnson had already pinned up in the classroom. One photo was of Brazilian soldiers going off to war. One of them looked a bit like Daddy. As Bone ran a finger over its glossy surface, she wondered where he was now. Would these fellas run into him? Bone was studying the other pictures—looking for familiar faces—when Will rapped on the back door.

Before she could move, Will entered and placed the jelly jar on the table in front of her.

Please read it, his eyes said. He longed to know everything about his daddy. Bone could see that in his eyes, too. She'd also ached to find out all she could about Mama.

Bone held her hand above it. She still felt that pull. It was warm like an ember but it made her feel hollow. The fire inside snuffed out all the air in the jar. And it pulled in sounds like moth to a flame. Could it trap her, too? What if she touched it and couldn't find her way back out? She yanked her hand away and shook her head. Not yet at least.

"We still got the baseball game," she said. "And maybe we ought to talk to some more people—like Mamaw—or your mother."

Will snatched the jar off the table and stuffed it in his pocket. He scribbled out a note and held it in front of her.

No good comes from talking.

Bone sat back in her chair, confused and frankly a bit stung by the remark. He may not talk—but she sure did. It was her best thing. One of them, at least. But there was an old saying: Talk is silver, but silence is gold.

"Hey, Will," Mrs. Price said as she walked into the kitchen. "I'm plumb out of cookies. But we got corn bread. Can I get you a piece? Or coffee maybe?"

Will shook his head as he stuck the note back in his pocket. He tipped his hat and left.

"Did you two have a fight?" Mrs. Price asked. It was very unusual for Will to turn down Mrs. Price's cooking.

"I'm not sure," Bone said. Will would go to the baseball game and try out the jar. He loved baseball almost more than anything. But he didn't want to talk to Mamaw—or maybe it was his mother he was afraid to talk to. Maybe Bone needed to do his talking for him like she used to.

Mrs. Price kissed Bone on the top of the head and went upstairs.

The sounds of *Father Flanagan's Boys Town* drifted in from the parlor. The show wasn't Bone's favorite. They were mostly true stories about the orphans. But Uncle Junior liked it. Uncle Junior! He was there, too, when Will's daddy died. He might know a piece of the puzzle. Bone packed up her homework and took it into the parlor.

"Uncle Junior?" she asked. His head was nodding as he sat in Daddy's chair by the fire. The newspaper had slipped out of his hands.

"Hmm?" He snapped awake.

"Were you in the mines the day Will's father died?" Bone sat on the hearth. She knew he was. He hadn't missed work in thirty years.

"Yes, I was. Why?" Junior looked at her peculiarly. "Are you worried about Will?"

"What happened?" She set her homework aside.

"Well, it was an ordinary enough day." Uncle Junior leaned forward in his chair. "We had a lot more men working back then. Four or five shafts were being dug at a time. Me and your daddy

91

were dynamiting a new shaft. William and Scotty were reclaiming lumber plumb on the other end of the mine in one of the old sections. It was lunchtime. And me and Bay were talking about football. The Giants had whupped the Eagles the night before. I was eating a slice of Evelyn's pecan pie." Uncle Junior closed his eyes for a moment as he savored the memory.

Bone didn't really remember Aunt Evelyn; she'd died a year or so before Mama did.

Junior's eyes flashed open again. "Then the mine rumbled. We hadn't had an accident in ages, not like when I first started working in the mines as a kid. We scrambled up to the mantrip. It wasn't until we got to the surface and took a count did we know William and Scotty were missing. Me, your daddy, Chuck Whitaker, and a few others went back down. Shaft twenty-three had collapsed, but we could hear something. After we powdered down the area, we commenced to digging, too. It took us a few hours and a change of shift to get through. Scotty was pinned under a beam, which saved him from getting crushed worse than he did. William was farther back."

"They were eating lunch, too," Bone said matter-of-factly.

"I expect so. We all stop at noon and eat right there in the cut." Then it came to Junior. "Bone, is this because you touched Will's dinner bucket?" Junior had seen Bone's reaction that day when he thrust the pail into her hands. That was before he knew for sure she had a Gift. "Did you see William's . . . death?"

Bone nodded. She'd seen the darkness and much more falling on Will's dad.

"Oh, Bone. I should've put two and two together." Junior sank back in the chair. "I told Mama that day I thought your Gift was coming on, but I didn't give much thought to what you were actually seeing."

"Mr. Scott said you gave him the dinner bucket. Why didn't Mrs. Kincaid keep it?" Bone asked.

"Sarah didn't want it in the house for some reason. She wouldn't say why," Uncle Junior said. "So Scotty, Bay, and me decided we'd keep the dinner bucket for Will, seeing as it was also his granddaddy's." Junior yawned mightily. "Funny thing, that dinner bucket was banged up a bit—but we found William holding on to this empty jelly jar. Not a scratch on it."

Bone shivered. Will's daddy died with that damn jelly jar in his hand. Was the jar haunted? Somehow that didn't feel right. But something happened in those last moments to give the jar power. And Bone did not want to see what that was.

UNCLE ASH WASN'T too hard to convince when it came down to it. He was a baseball fan just like everyone else in the coal camps. Uncle Junior wrangled one of the mine trucks to take the Big Vein team over to the minor league game in Pulaski. Will played right field for the miners. Even Aunt Mattie decided to go, seeing as it was a war bond drive, so she drove Mamaw and Ruby in their big black Ford. That left Bone and Uncle Ash in his truck, which suited them both just fine. They'd all meet up with Uncle Junior's daughters at the game. The trip was only forty miles, but Bone had never been to a semipro game.

Uncle Ash turned the radio down as they got onto the main road. "Bone, I've been thinking . . ." He lit a cigarette and rolled down the window partway. "If you practice on objects I know the history of, I can at least help you sort out what happened when. Look in the glove box." It was more of a flap than a box.

Bone opened it and pulled out a leather dog collar. It had the name Myrtle tooled into the leather. It was warm to the touch, even though the truck was cold. Bone closed her eyes and saw a dog running through the woods, barking for the pure joy of it. The happy was strong in this object.

"She was my first dog, one that was just mine. Daddy and Junior had hunting dogs, and I took care of them. Daddy gave her to me as a pup for my eighth birthday. See if you can find that memory."

Bone ran a finger over the name. Images swirled by her, all mixed up like eddies in a river. A pup digging gleefully in Mamaw's garden. An old dog sunning herself on the treehouse porch, Ash scratching her ear. A young Ash wading through the river, Myrtle paddling close behind. One memory didn't stand out as happier or sadder than the others. Bone traced the name again as she searched for an image of an eight-year-old Ash among the currents. *When did he carve this?* she silently asked. Suddenly, she could see a young Ash working the letters and the little flourishes into the leather with a hammer and chisel. He stuck his tongue in the corner of his mouth as he pounded the leather. A little black pup dropped a stick at his feet. He absently threw it and the dog skittered after it.

Uncle Ash was right. Asking the object a question really helped!

Bone laid the collar in her lap. "Uncle Ash, did she—" She didn't want to see something happen to Myrtle.

"Don't worry. She lived to a ripe old age and wasn't wearing the collar when she passed." He flicked the ashes off his Lucky out the window.

Bone picked the collar up again and described what she saw as the truck passed by the road that went up to the new ammunition plant in Radford. The army had begun building it when the war started. The soldiers guarding the gate waved at Ash.

"What do you see next?" he asked as he waved back.

Bone heard distant rumbles of thunder and saw flashes of light. She felt blind terror from the dog as she raced to an older Ash—and then reassuring comfort as Myrtle pressed her body against Ash's leg and he patted her head. "She was afraid of thunderstorms," Bone announced.

"Yes, I'd forgotten about that." Uncle Ash rolled his window down all the way.

"Poor Myrtle!" Bone now felt a wave of sadness as she watched a teenage Ash get on a bus and drive away. "You left her to go to war!"

"Dumbest thing I ever done." Uncle Ash shook his head as he fished in his pocket for another Lucky.

"But you came back." Bone felt Myrtle's frenzied happiness when Ash returned. The dog's other memories and feelings were not as crystal clear as a person's. Myrtle's were a blur of activity: eating, chasing things through the woods, barking at other things, wading in the creek, eating some more. Once she'd found that first memory, though, Bone could generally follow the current of Myrtle's life.

Then the memories became human again. Ash was still a young man, only now he had that familiar, easygoing sadness about him. She could feel his heartbreak as he slipped the collar off his beloved dog's neck and held her. Her muzzle was gray, and her breathing heavy. Ash laid his hand on her and took it away.

"*Nothing you can do, Ash,*" Mamaw said. "*She's just old, and it's her time.*"

Young man Ash took a draught from Mamaw's hand and gently poured it down Myrtle's throat. Her breathing eased. Ash cradled the dog's head in his lap, clutching the collar in one hand, until she slipped away. He cried as he sang a song to her about packing up your troubles.

With a catch in her voice, Bone told her uncle what she was seeing. He nodded and handed her a hankie. She blew her nose before putting the collar back in the glove box.

"There's some peppermint sticks in there, too."

Bone rooted in the tiny compartment and found a small paper sack with the candy in it, under another pack of Lucky Strikes, a box of matches, ration books, and some work gloves.

She sucked on a peppermint stick. Using her Gift took some energy out of her, though not as much as it first did, and the candy helped. Uncle Ash had taught her that. And now he'd also taught her to navigate the currents of an object's memory a bit better.

"Was the collar trying to show you something in particular?" Uncle Ash asked.

She hadn't asked the collar that question. But as she thought on it, the song crept back into her mind. "What's a kit bag?" Bone asked.

"It's what soldiers put their uniforms and gear in. Why?" He blew smoke out the open window.

"That's what you were singing to Myrtle." She handed the handkerchief back to her uncle. "'Pack up your troubles in your old kit bag, and smile, smile, smile.'" She sang it way off-key on purpose.

Ash chuckled. "I was? It was a popular song back then. We sang it on the boat coming back. It was probably the only song I knew all the way through." Uncle Ash took a last drag on his Lucky Strike and then ground it out on the side mirror of the truck. "Guess that's not strictly true. I loved that dog, but I wasn't just crying for her. It was like I'd packed up all my troubles in that kit bag and hadn't let them out until then." Uncle Ash pulled out his dog tags. The metal discs hung on a strap of leather around his neck. He always wore them, as far as she knew, but she'd never thought to ask him about them.

She wondered what she'd see if she touched them. Considering what the war had done to him, she didn't wonder about it long. What had her Gift been trying to tell her about the dog collar?

Uncle Ash quickly tucked them back into his shirt. "I wouldn't touch these if I were you." He winked at her and then turned up the radio. "Ever."

It belted out, "I got spurs that jingle, jangle, jingle . . ."

It was an awful song.

Bone and Ash sang along, each trying to out-awful the other, until they got to the stadium.

11

THE PULASKI COUNTS' stadium was far grander than Centennial Ballpark where the miners played. The Counts were semipro. Some of the players even made it to the major leagues. Bone thought the Counts was a dumb name for a ball team. Then she read the plaque out front while Uncle Ash got their tickets. Evidently Casimir Pulaski was a real live Polish count who was one of George Washington's generals in the Continental Army. The count whupped the British on the battlefield.

The mine truck rolled up and Uncle Junior let the team out. Actually, Bone noticed as they all marched out of the truck, only the white players came.

"Where's Tiny and Oscar?" Bone asked Uncle Junior. He looked a bit uncomfortable.

Uncle Ash pointed to the sign over the entrance.

WHITES ONLY

"That's not fair," Bone said. Mr. Sherman and Mr. Fears both worked in the mines and played on the mine team alongside white folks. It was peculiar that the men and their families didn't live in Big Vein, now that Bone thought about it. The black folk had their own community over in Sherman's Forest. Did they have a choice about that? Bone wondered. If not, that wasn't fair either.

"No, it is not," Uncle Ash said as he pointed her in the right direction. "A lot of things in that regard ain't fair," he added.

Mamaw, Aunt Mattie, Ruby, Ivy, and Fern were waiting for them inside the gates. Uncle Junior hugged his girls before the womenfolk headed off toward the stands. Fern's husband had to work, but he'd bought them good seats.

Bone, her uncles, and the boys of the Big Vein ball team made their way to the left field bleachers. They were only half full. Garvin and Marvin Linkous jabbered on about baseball, the world series, and big league players joining up for the war. Will nodded at the appropriate times, but Bone could see he was clutching something in his coat pocket close to him as he walked.

The jelly jar.

❧

The speaker above them squawked. "Welcome to the Pulaski Counts' stadium! I want to thank you all for coming to our special war bond drive—and our final game. It's my sad duty to announce that, after today, the Virginia League is suspending play for the duration of the war. Most of our players have already gone and signed up to fight. So we're having this game to send 'em off in style!"

The crowd groaned.

"Aw nuts," one of the boys exclaimed.

"I heard on the radio that the big leagues might suspend play, too," Uncle Ash commented.

Will looked stricken.

"Please stand for our national anthem," the announcer said.

"This is new," Uncle Junior said as he got to his feet. "They always played the 'Banner' during the seventh-inning stretch."

"Majors started doing it on account of the war," Uncle Ash said just before "The Star-Spangled Banner" played over the speakers. It was on a scratchy record.

Bone sang along, trying this time not to be awful. It didn't really work. All during the song, she was wondering what else could get suspended *for the duration*.

After they sat down, Garvin Linkous asked Uncle Junior, "Mr. Reed, is the Miners' League gonna have to stop playing, too?"

Will turned alarmed eyes to Junior.

"I don't know yet, boys. Depends on if the mines have enough men to field teams. We're already running out of folks to work second shift." He signaled the vendor to throw him two bags of roasted peanuts. The bags sailed over the boys' heads, right into Uncle Junior's hands. He tossed back a coin.

Marvin nodded. "I heard a couple of the fellas say they're signing up."

"We'd sign up if we were eighteen," Garvin added. The twins were only sixteen.

Not even baseball was safe from the war.

～∂～

Throughout the game, Bone watched Will while she shelled and munched warm peanuts. He'd get caught up in the action, then touch his pocket, look around, and go back to the game. During the seventh-inning stretch, Will excused himself. He gave Uncle Junior a sign that made him laugh.

"That's a good idear," he said as he followed Will out.

"Take Me Out to the Ball Game" started playing over the speakers. When the chorus came around, the crowd joined in. The stretch was Bone's favorite part of the game. Everyone got up and moved around. Now there was singing! "'Buy me some peanuts and Cracker Jack,'" Bone crooned at Uncle Ash. Together, they tried to out-awful each other again. It was a tie.

Uncle Junior came back before the end of the stretch—but Will didn't.

"Oh, he went for pop," Uncle Junior explained. "He, um, made room for it first." Her uncle chuckled.

Will still hadn't returned to his seat by the top of the eighth. Bone eventually spotted him, though, sitting high up in the bleachers under a speaker, with his hand in his jacket pocket. Not a soul was near him, and he didn't have a soda pop either.

The announcer came on in the bottom of the eighth. "Next up is Pulaski's own Bernie Teague. If he gets a homer, he'll set a new league record. Tomorrow, he ships out to the marines." Everyone was on the edge of their seats when Teague came up to bat. The whole stadium was silent as a grave. Bone could hear the player knock his cleats clean with the bat before he stepped up to the plate. Bone watched Will.

He reached into his pocket and slowly unscrewed the lid of the jar. The pitcher threw one right down the middle. The bat cracked against the ball, sending it over the infield fence. "He tattooed that one!" the announcer shouted. Will quickly screwed the lid back on and stuffed it into his coat pocket. He had a huge grin on his face as he looked down at Bone.

The speaker crackled, and the crowd roared. Everyone shot to their feet. Will whipped around to watch Teague round the bases.

As the speaker above them crackled again, the man in front of Bone cursed loudly. "These darn speakers are always breaking."

They could still hear the center-field speakers okay—except when Pulaski caught a pop fly to end the game in the ninth. Then the cheering of the crowd drowned out everything else.

Bone, her uncles, and the boys emerged from the stadium to find Mattie and Ruby going at it again across the parking lot. Bone hadn't noticed them leaving their seats before the end of the game. Their voices carried right far.

"Oh lord," Uncle Junior muttered. "You boys get in the truck." He tossed Will the keys before he headed toward the fracas. Will and the other miners ambled toward their truck, which was parked in the shade near Uncle Ash's pickup.

Uncle Ash unrolled a half-empty bag of peanuts and passed it to Bone. Together, they cracked peanut shells as they watched the row unfold.

Mamaw was standing between Mattie and Ruby now, with Fern and Ivy backing Ruby up. Uncle Junior's grown daughters towered over their younger cousin.

"Young lady, we have to live somewhere," Aunt Mattie hollered.

Ruby turned her back on her mother.

"Don't you dare," Aunt Mattie huffed. "You *will* speak to me!"

"Thanks for the offer," Ruby told Fern in a loud, but civil voice. "Tell Mother I will get a ride home," she added icily. She pushed past Uncle Junior just as he reached the group of women.

"What'd you think that's all about?" Bone asked Uncle Ash.

"I expect Fern asked Mattie and Ruby to move in with them come January, at least until they figure out what they're going to do." Uncle Ash pulled out his own truck keys. "That was the plan, at least. That's why Mama got Mattie to come today."

"That's nice of Fern!" Bone was happy Ruby had someplace to go—and it was a nice place. Cousin Fern and her husband had a great big house in Radford near the hospital. But that would mean Ruby would have to go to school there. Bone felt a little less happy about that.

"Yes, it was, but I'm guessing it won't be as easy as that." Uncle Ash pointed at Ruby steaming toward them. "Best say goodbye to Will and quick."

Bone ran to catch up to Will. "I can meet you at the cemetery after supper," she whispered.

He looked at her blankly.

"You know, to listen to it." She pointed to his coat pocket.

Will stuck his hand in the pocket and hesitated. Then he shook his head and jumped in the back of the truck.

It hit Bone like a bolt out of the blue. He'd never *not* wanted to do something with her. Ever since they were little, they'd done everything together. School. Fishing. Swimming in the river. Summer movies on the croquet field. He even went with Bone to help Mamaw in the garden or out foraging in the woods. They did things by themselves, of course, like him working in the mines. But he'd never said no to her before. She wasn't sure how to feel about it, but it worried her.

Ruby stomped past. "I may have to live with her, but that doesn't mean I have to talk to her." She climbed into the cab of Uncle Ash's truck. Bone and Uncle Ash exchanged a glance that said, *It's gonna be a long ride*. Bone slid wearily into the passenger's seat next to Ruby. Uncle Ash lit a smoke before he sat in the driver's seat.

After they pulled out onto the main road, Uncle Ash spoke. "Ruby, honey, do you want to talk about it?"

"Don't pretend you care," she snapped, her eyes straight ahead.

"Ruby! That ain't no way to talk to Uncle Ash," Bone snapped back. "Stop being ugly!" She knew she was really more mad at Will than Ruby, but still no one should talk to Uncle Ash like that.

Ruby stared at Bone for a long, hard moment. "Sorry," she grudgingly said to Ash. "She just makes me so mad."

Bone knew the feeling well. But when Ruby said it, it was like the pot calling the kettle black.

"Oh, I know." Uncle Ash chuckled. "Willow used to keep the peace between me and Mattie. I expect Henry did the same for you two."

"Nobody likes Mother." Ruby crossed her arms and scowled straight ahead.

Neither Ash nor Bone could argue with that.

"Doesn't mean I don't love her, though," Ash said. "It's a hard thing loving someone we don't particularly like."

"Amen," Bone added.

"But we do it." Uncle Ash looked at Bone when he said this.

Ruby's scowl deepened. "Well, I'm not talking to her—and please, please let's do that thing on Halloween." She whispered that last part at Bone.

The ride home took forever and a day.

Bone wasn't sure who she was more worried about, Will or Ruby. At least she understood what Ruby was feeling. Maybe.

12

WILL DIDN'T COME over after dinner. He always did. Bone was torn between being mad and worried. Worried won.

Bone slipped on her sweater and ran over to the Kincaids' house. Mrs. Kincaid was sweeping the porch with a distracted fury.

"Bone?" Mrs. Kincaid stopped sweeping.

"Is Will here?"

"He went for his walk a while ago." She leaned on her broom and peered at Bone through the darkness. Mrs. Kincaid looked like she was tied up in a knot inside. "I thought he always ended up at your place."

He usually did. Bone had a dark feeling she knew where he was. His mother looked worried, too, but Bone wasn't about to tell her that Will was at the cemetery. Again. That would not make his mother feel one jot better.

"Maybe he ran into one of the boys and they're talking baseball," Bone said.

Mrs. Kincaid relaxed. "That's what it is." She nodded. "Baseball, always baseball with that boy." She started sweeping again.

Bone turned to leave and then thought better of it. "Ma'am, do you mind if I ask you a question?"

"Of course not, honey." She kept sweeping.

"When did Will stop talking?" Bone asked quietly.

Mrs. Kincaid swept a little harder. Bone thought she hadn't heard her. Then she stopped. "Right after his daddy's funeral. Why?" She put one hand on her hip and stared at Bone.

Bone shrugged. "Just curious." Both of them knew there was more to Will not talking than that—only Will's mother didn't want to say, and Bone didn't know how to ask.

Mrs. Kincaid went back to sweeping.

❧

The idea of going to the cemetery after dark gave Bone the willies. She didn't believe in ghosts, devil dogs, or Jack ma lanterns . . . exactly. Daddy said that was all nonsense. They made good stories. Scary stories. But Will was up there with that jelly jar talking to his dead father at night—near Halloween. Bone shivered.

She went back to the boardinghouse to get a flashlight from the back porch. Mrs. Price had bought it for use in blackouts. The ad in *Life* magazine said every house needed to have at least one in case the Germans got this far. It felt new, like no one had ever touched it or left a memory on its cardboard-and-metal body. It was a relief. Bone kept the light off until she got to the gravel drive up to the graveyard. She wasn't about to creep through the woods and into the cemetery the back way, especially in the dark. That would be too much like the nightmare she kept having about Daddy lost in a forest somewhere. Once or twice, though, she flicked on the light to peer into the trees or into the shadows by someone's porch. And once she could swear she saw a flicker of light where there shouldn't have been. *It's just foxfire,* she told herself. *Not Jack and his lantern. Foxfire.* Mamaw had taught her certain mushrooms gave off a glow deep in the woods around this time of year. *That's foxfire, just foxfire. Not ghost lights or will-o'-the-wisps or Jack ma lanterns. Foxfire.*

Bone stood between the two stone posts that had once held the gates. They didn't seem like hardly enough to keep the spirits in, if there were such a thing, or grave robbers out. She took a deep breath and peered into the cemetery with her flashlight. Every ghost story she'd ever heard was running through her head. And some of them happened at night in a graveyard. Like the one about the ghost horse and rider galloping up the road and into the cemetery, where they disappeared without a sound or hoofprint.

A twig snapped.

Bone gulped hard and flashed the light around her. Nothing.

"They're just stories," she told herself as she stepped into the graveyard.

A light flickered in the woods. Then Bone heard the rumble of a mine truck rounding the bend in the road. Headlights.

As she picked her way up the path, she could see a figure sitting on the bench. Bone clicked off her light. She heard the sounds of the baseball game, the train, the dogs, the crickets, and the radio. In the darkness, they flitted around Will's head like dim fireflies. Then she heard a child's high voice followed by a man's raspy, low one. Bone couldn't tell what it said. Will closed the jar and opened it again. The sounds flew around him again and again as Bone crept closer, straining to hear. Each time Will leaned in toward the end to hear the man's words.

Was that his father? Was that child Will? She felt like an intruder on a very private and unearthly conversation.

Bone backed noiselessly out of the cemetery. She definitely needed to talk to Mamaw about this.

13

The faded yellow pickup truck was waiting for Bone after school. Uncle Ash held the door open for her with a flourish. "Your chariot awaits, Forever Girl."

Bone clambered up into the truck. When Uncle Ash threw it in gear, glass rattled around in the back as the truck bumped down the road toward the river.

"I had calls to make in Big Vein," Uncle Ash said absently, his mind a million miles away. He shook it off. "One of them was a stumper. How was school?"

"Boring—as usual. Particularly the math lesson," Bone replied. Corolla snuggled into her lap.

Uncle Ash chuckled. "Get the schooling while you can. India, I mean Miss Spencer, says you could easily go to college with your brains, maybe become a professor like her someday."

"Really?" Bone had thoroughly enjoyed helping Miss Spencer collect stories at the beginning of the school year. So had Uncle Ash.

The truck pulled up to the ferry crossing.

Mr. Goodwin, who operated the ferry, had seen them coming down the road. He was halfway across the river.

"How 'bout another type of lesson?" Ash asked. "Fetch that little book out of the glove box."

Bone undid the flap. Underneath the pack of smokes and paper sack of peppermint was a thin, faded brown book. Bone couldn't recall seeing Uncle Ash doing much reading—except for the newspaper and maybe a few textbooks on animals. Bone picked up the little book gingerly. It fell open to a spot marked by a letter. Bone recognized Miss Spencer's neat handwriting on the envelope—and the return address said Swannanoa Hall, Hollins College, Roanoke, Virginia. Bone touched the envelope and almost blushed.

"What do you see?" Uncle Ash asked, his eyes still on the road.

She saw Miss Spencer sitting at a wooden desk, surrounded by shelves and shelves of books and old objects, writing away. Occasionally, she'd glance at another letter, this one with Uncle Ash's chicken scratch on it. A pleasant, warm feeling radiated off the pages like an old sweater.

"She really likes you," Bone said with a grin.

"What?" Uncle Ash looked at her—and then a deep blush colored his face. "Dang it! I forgot that was in there."

Bone offered him the envelope, which he snatched up and stuffed into his shirt pocket.

"She does?" he asked, a little smile replacing the blush. "Back to the book. What's it telling you?"

"Uh-huh," Bone replied. She held the book quietly. *What is your secret?*

She didn't see much at first. She could tell the book was Ash's. She turned it over in her hands. Its spine was cracked, and a tiny ribbon attached to the book marked his place. The cover said *The Poems of John McCrae.* Poems? Bone looked at Uncle Ash. He merely raised an eyebrow.

Bone closed her eyes and asked again. She could see her uncle stretched out in the back of the truck, his boots on the tailgate, dogs sprawled around him. The warm breeze tasted of salt. Waves crashed against the beach. There were other sounds she couldn't quite make out. And Uncle Ash was reading the book aloud to himself. She felt a mixture of sadness and peace as the waves and the words drowned out the other sounds. She could hear them more clearly now. Guns, explosions, and screams.

"In Flanders Fields . . . ," Uncle Ash started to recite from memory.

Mr. Goodwin rapped on the hood of the car.

Bone dropped the book.

Uncle Ash hopped out and grabbed the bowline to tie off the ferry. "Keep reading," he hollered at Bone.

She did not want to hear the other sounds again.

Instead, she stuffed the book back into the glove box. She and the dogs knew the drill. They climbed out of the car and onto the rickety little ferry. It was only big enough for one car and a couple people. Uncle Ash drove the truck onto the bobbing platform. Then Mr. Goodwin untied the bowline again and threw the lever, sending the ferry lurching back toward the other shore. Mr. Goodwin nodded to Bone, accepted a cigarette from Uncle Ash, and then stood at the bow of his ferry. The winch motor ground its gears loudly as it pulled the ferry across the water.

Bone and her uncle leaned against the warm hood of the truck. In a hushed voice, she told him what she'd seen—but not what she'd heard. Mr. Goodwin couldn't hear them over the groaning motor, but she didn't want to take a chance. "Why poetry?" she asked in a normal voice.

"John McCrae was a surgeon in my battalion during the Great War. He wrote the poem about Flanders Fields after he saw his friend die." Ash took a long drag on his cigarette and then blew an imperfect smoke ring.

"I didn't see any of that," Bone whispered.

"Oh, I got the book after the war," Ash said quickly. "I wouldn't give you anything that had actually been in the war," he added quietly. He shook his head and tucked his dog tags back into his flannel shirt. "The poem captured something about the war, something only a body who'd been there might see."

"You read that when you hear the guns in your head," Bone told him. And the screaming.

Uncle Ash practically spun around to look at her. "What? You could see . . ." He leaned back against the truck again. "Oh, Forever Girl, you do have quite a Gift!"

Bone had to agree. She was surprised, too, at how much she'd seen—and heard. When the Gift first came on, back in the summer, she'd only been able to experience the truly awful or truly wonderful memories in an object. Now, those powerful memories were surprising her less and less. She hadn't even had to use Uncle Ash's gloves. And she was seeing quieter memories, like Uncle Ash reading poetry.

The ferry bumped into the Dry Branch side of the river. Uncle Ash handed her a peppermint stick as they climbed back into the truck and waved their goodbyes to Mr. Goodwin. Bone held the faded little book in her hand one more time. This time she could see a younger Ash, maybe in his twenties, unwrapping a plain brown package, postmarked Chicago. Inside was a shining new book—and no note.

"Someone sent it to you!"

"Can you see who?" Ash asked.

She shook her head. Many hands had touched it from wherever it was published to Chicago and then through the mail. None of them really cared for the book, though, not like

Ash. Bone had a feeling whoever sent the book never actually touched it.

"Nuts, I was hoping you could!" Instead of another Lucky, Uncle Ash stuck a stick of candy in his mouth.

They drove up the road to Reed Mountain, each thinking their own thoughts and relishing the restorative wonders of Red Bird peppermint.

✦

Once they'd gotten to the Reed place, Uncle Ash dropped Bone off in front of Mamaw's "office," as she liked to call it. It was a little cabin down below the main house where she made her herbal medicines. Most of the flowers, herbs, and vegetables were gone from the gardens that surrounded the cabin. The earth was neatly turned over, waiting for next spring. Only the squash, pumpkins, and dark leafy greens were left. The hay across the way was baled. The trees behind the cabin were ablaze with oranges and reds, except for the dark greens of the Virginia pines. The breeze smelled of woodsmoke, hay, and a hint of compost. Bone missed the lavenders and rosemaries of summer.

Inside the cabin, though, it smelled like jam. Bone drank in the aroma. The cabin was one large open room with several workbenches. Mamaw's office always reminded Bone of a mad scientist's lab from the movies. Tubes, drying racks, and other contraptions filled every surface. The walls were lined with shelves, each packed with jars, bottles, and little paper sacks. Bundles of drying herbs hung from the rafters. A large table sat in the center. Across the room, Mamaw stood over the woodstove stirring a pot and humming. Her calico cat, Sassafras, was curled up in the chair by the stove.

"You're just in time to help me make the elderberry syrup." She nodded to the closest workbench.

Bone knew the drill. This workbench had the jars, strainers, cheesecloth, and a contraption for squeezing the juice out of the berries and herbs. "Can I work the press?"

"I was hoping you would." Mamaw carried the pot over to the bench. "My grip is not what it was."

Bone spun open the top of the homemade press and lined the bottom with the cheesecloth. She pulled a rubber hose over the spigot on the bottom and placed a jar underneath. She put a strainer over the top. Maneuvering the pot over the open press, Mamaw poured in the burbling mixture of cooked elderberries, cloves, cinnamon, and garlic. The pungent steam filled the room with a sweet and spicy aroma.

"Smells glorious, doesn't it?" She set the pot down and grabbed the strainer, which caught all the bits of the herbs. She inhaled. "Smells like fall to me."

"Smells like pie," Bone replied. Every year Mamaw made pints of elderberry syrup as well as jam and tinctures. This was Mamaw's busy season, preserving the fruits of her gardens and making them into herbal medicines—and food, but mostly medicine. She and Uncle Ash also foraged for wild plants and mushrooms on their many acres of forest. The drying racks were full of berries, flowers, roots, and leaves. Out back, Bone knew she'd find more of the same.

"Like harvesttime." Mamaw hummed as she lined up clean jars in a neat row. "Bet you didn't know Halloween started as a harvest festival."

Bone did. Mamaw told her that every time they did this. Back in Scotland and Ireland, in the old days, they celebrated the end of the lighter half of the year and the beginning of the dark half on October 31.

Bone got up on a stool and cranked the press closed—and kept cranking. The warm juice trickled down through the hose and into the jar, filling it halfway with dark purple liquid. Mamaw replaced the jars as Bone cranked.

"So what's on your mind?" Mamaw asked.

Bone kept cranking. Finally she said, "I'm worried about Will."

Mamaw slid another jar under the hose. "Really? I thought that boy could take care of himself better than anyone."

"Do you remember when he stopped talking?" Bone put her weight into turning the handle.

"Yes, it was right after his daddy died. Sarah brought him to me and Willow after she took him to the doctor in Roanoke." Mamaw put another jar under the hose.

Bone stopped cranking. "Mama saw him?" She wiped her forehead on her sweater sleeve. For a second, she saw Mama touching a boy's throat in this very room. Mama shook her head.

"Yes, she didn't see anything wrong with him—physically."

Bone started cranking again. If nothing was wrong, did Will just choose not to talk? *No good comes from talking.* Or was it the jar? It had to be the jar.

"That doctor in Roanoke said it was all in his head—on account of losing his daddy. I always figured he'd talk when he was good and ready." Mamaw squeezed the last bit of elderberry juice out of the hose and motioned for Bone to stop. "Okay, that's all there is—for this batch." She filled each jar the rest of the way with honey. It was from the hive she kept out in the woods. Then she stirred each jar before putting on a lid. She handed Bone a spoonful from the final jar. "My mama always said a spoonful a day of this keeps the doctor away."

Bone licked the sweet berry mixture clean. It had a tang to it that made the berries all the sweeter. "You should make hard candy out of this."

"That's certainly an idea." Mamaw stood and stretched her back. "There's gonna be a shortage of candy come Halloween, I fear. But some would rather I make wine out of this berry. Hmmm, I could use some of the honey . . ." Mamaw started humming as she thought.

The back door swung open, and Corolla raced in, followed by Uncle Ash carrying a box full of mason jars. They were filled with a clear liquid. And they'd rattled in the back of the truck all the way up the mountain.

"Mr. Childress paid me in 'shine." He grinned as he set the box down on the counter. "This should pay him up and then some. His son-in-law Ronny said he'll try to distill you some more before he ships out."

Mamaw examined the jars and motioned for Ash to put them by the sink. Bone knew exactly what was in them. Mamaw and Ash didn't drink more than a beer or two at a baseball game, but she needed alcohol to make tinctures. And folks often paid their bills—for either Mamaw's or Uncle Ash's services—in trade.

"We might have to set up Hawthorne's old still again," Mamaw said with a shake of her head.

"Ronny's missus is wondering if you had something stronger than the chamomile tea for sleeping. She's working nights over at the powder plant and can't get to sleep during daylight."

"Bone, honey, fetch some valerian off the shelf. We can make her a tincture of that."

The herbs were arranged alphabetically in jars and packets along the front wall. Bone had almost forgotten just how many jars Mamaw had. She ran her finger along a shelf. None of the jars pulled at her like Will's did. Bone only got flashes of Mamaw doing exactly what she was doing now: intently and lovingly filling the jars, grinding herbs in the old coffee grinder, filling little bottles with tinctures, all the while humming to herself. Sometimes Mama or Bone or Uncle Ash were helping her, but mostly her only company was a long line of calico cats: Sassafras, Buttercup, Poppy, and ones born long before Bone. All of them were no doubt named after flowers or herbs. There was a lot of happy in these jars.

Bone found the valerian jar. She didn't open it because she knew it smelled like old socks, old socks that had been rotting in the rain for years.

"Have you asked her yet?" Uncle Ash asked Bone in a whisper when she returned to the counter. "About Will's . . ."

Bone shook her head. "I'm getting there," she whispered back.

"Ask me what?" Mamaw said from the stove. "You know I ain't deaf yet."

"You got better hearing than most teenagers, Mama," Ash said.

Bone put the valerian jar on the bench.

"Well?" Mamaw looked her square in the eye. Bone couldn't get out of asking it.

"Can an object have a Gift of its own?" Bone watched Mamaw for a reaction.

Mamaw motioned for Bone to pull up a stool. Uncle Ash poured himself and Mamaw a cup of coffee. She always kept a pot going on the woodstove when she worked. "There's a pop in the icebox for Bone," Mamaw told him and he dutifully fetched it—and a piece of carrot cake for them all to share. She waited until everyone was seated around the bench with a cup and the slice of cake to reply. "What do you mean, honey, about an object with a Gift?" Mamaw always took her questions seriously.

"Like it has a power to do something." Bone sipped her grape Nehi.

"What is the object exactly?" Mamaw stirred honey into her coffee without taking her eyes off Bone.

"A jelly jar. But I'm afraid to touch the thing." Bone stared at the valerian jar. "It pulls at me," Bone whispered.

"You're right not to touch it then." Mamaw took Bone's hand. "You got to foller your own lights, especially when it comes to your Gift."

Her own lights were telling Bone not to mess with the jelly jar.

"Do you think it's like that mirror I told you about?" Uncle Ash asked. "That's just a story." He cut off a piece of the cake and pushed it toward Bone.

Bone shrugged. She couldn't put it into words, and it frustrated her to no end.

"What Gift does this object have?" Mamaw asked, sipping her coffee.

"It catches sounds."

Mamaw about spit out her coffee.

Uncle Ash let out a low whistle and got up to pace a bit. "Will had a jelly jar at the cemetery the other day."

Bone nodded. "He got it with his daddy's dinner bucket," she admitted. She felt bad for telling on him, but she felt better, too. Will was acting stranger and stranger about the blame jar. "Uncle Junior said Mr. Kincaid died with the jar in his hand." Junior would no doubt tell Mamaw that Bone had been asking about Mr. Kincaid's death.

Uncle Ash stopped in his tracks.

Mamaw didn't say anything.

"I've heard plenty of stories about haunted objects," Ash finally said. "But all the ones about miners are usually friendly. The ghost of a dead miner is looking out after his buddies—or his son. If you believe in that kind of thing." Ash looked to his mother. "Mama, you're awfully quiet."

She took a long drink of coffee before she spoke. "I don't hold with the idea of haunted objects. A jar, you say?" She picked up one of the jars she'd just filled and peered at it before setting it down again. "I've heard of jars being used for spells and such. You put some herbs and liquid—water, vinegar, or honey—into the jar and then say some words. Honey is supposed to make someone sweet on you, for instance. In fact, I've sold plenty of herbs that were probably used for that kind of witchery." She took another long drink of coffee. "It's all bunk. Just like haints."

"What is it then?" Bone asked, exasperated. She set the pop bottle down on the table a little harder than she'd intended. She was glad it wasn't a haint or a spell, but what did that leave?

Mamaw leaned in. "Strong emotions leave memories on objects; that's what you read with your Gift."

127

Bone nodded. It wasn't just what happened to the object she saw—but what happened to the person or animal it touched. That's what lingered after they were gone. They left imprints for her to see.

"My potions and herbs aren't any good just sitting on the shelf bottled up. You got to let 'em out and use them. You keep 'em in the jar too long, they're not good anymore. Or worse, they turn into poison. Maybe objects is like people. They can bottle up all that emotion that's best let out or it festers. Maybe a strong enough emotion can transform an object, give it some kind of power."

"William was trapped," Uncle Ash said. His voice was ragged around the edges. He took a deep breath as he stroked the dog tags around his neck. "Being trapped under all that earth, expecting to die, is a powerful dark feeling. If anything could transform an object, that could." He tucked his dog tags back in his shirt. He fumbled in his pocket for a cigarette.

Uncle Ash had been trapped in a collapsed tunnel during the last war, the so-called War to End all Wars. He didn't talk about it much.

"You lived through that," Bone said with a shiver. She'd seen just a few seconds of what Mr. Kincaid experienced. If that was what Uncle Ash had lived through for days, he was so much incredibly stronger than folks gave him credit for.

"I did, Forever Girl," Ash said quietly. "We had a bit more breathing space than William and Scotty had."

Mamaw rose from her stool and laid a hand on Uncle Ash's shoulder. Then she went back to the stove to pour herself another cup of coffee.

Both Uncle Ash and Mr. Kincaid had gone through something so awful Bone couldn't imagine it. And Mr. Kincaid had died. Still, she couldn't figure how that experience could give an ordinary object that power. What emotion could he have put into the jar to make it catch sounds like the radio and the dogs barking?

"Forever Girl, you do have a peculiar Gift," Uncle Ash said after he'd lit his smoke. "Come on, Bone, I'll run you home." He motioned toward the door. He was obviously done talking about this, but he paused on the threshold. "By the way, Mama, I need something for Mr. Childress's dogs. I saw them before I picked Bone up." He shook his head like something had stumped him. "Maybe some raw honey would do the trick."

"What was wrong with them?" Bone asked. They'd seemed just fine when Bone and Will had seen them in Flat Woods last Sunday.

"Darned if I know," Ash said as he held the door for Mamaw and Corolla. "They lost their voices, and I couldn't see a thing wrong with them."

Bone gasped. Mamaw turned on her heel and looked at Bone. Mr. Childress's dogs' voices had been one of the sounds they'd captured in the jar. That jar did more than record sounds. It stole them!

"Oh no," Bone said. She told them about her and Will's experiments.

"You best tell Will to keep a lid on that jar of his until you get to the bottom of this." Mamaw pointed the honey bottle in Bone's direction.

"Me?"

Mamaw nodded.

This was Bone's Gift, and she had to figure out how to use it.

14

HONEY BOTTLE STILL in hand, Mamaw studied Bone a few seconds and then asked, "Why don't you stay to supper?" She did not wait for Bone to answer. "Ash, run up to the house and call Mrs. Price."

The house was only about a few hundred feet away—and one story up from the cabin. The main Reed house was a magnificent, four-bedroom tree house astride four large oaks. Family legend was that Great-great-granddaddy Rowan built it before the Civil War. Bone adored the place.

"Sure thing," Uncle Ash said. He whistled and Corolla followed him out the door.

"Bone, fetch me that ledger off that shelf over yonder." She pointed to the high shelf over the dried teas and tinctures. "It's the big skinny book with the tree on the front."

Mamaw poured honey into her coffee and stirred it. Bone could hear the spoon slowly clinking against the cup like a ticking clock as she shooed Sassafras off the chair in the corner. She dragged it over to the shelf and hopped onto it. The ledger was wedged between one of Mamaw's books on plants and a *Gray's Anatomy*. That had been one of Mama's nursing books. Bone grabbed the skinny book by the spine—and the room began to turn a little. She saw Mamaw writing in the book—and many other women of all ages doing the same. Bone clutched the back of the chair to steady herself.

Mamaw was at her elbow in a flash. "Sorry, honey, I should've warned you. My mind was elsewhere." She steered Bone to the table. "What did you see?"

Bone slid onto the stool, still holding on to the ledger. The eddies of time swirled around her. Closing her eyes, she asked the images to calm themselves. They obliged. Then she could see each of the women more clearly. One was Great-grandma Daisy. Another was her mother. Or maybe her grandmother. This book had passed through so many generations of Reed women. "Nothing bad. Just a lot of strong-minded women owned this over the years." Bone was rather pleased she'd managed to control the book's powerful memories, even if just a little bit.

Laughing, Mamaw retrieved her cup of coffee and sat down next to Bone. "Yes, this is the family book. One woman from each generation keeps track of everyone's Gift. Someday, it'll be yours," she added matter-of-factly.

"Me?" Bone ran her finger across the tree etched in the fading leather. Closing her eyes, she could see bits and pieces of the women's stories. One was a water witch. Another could sense the weather. Several worked with herbs. *What do you want to show me?* One sketched an object she held in her hand. "Someone else had my Gift!" Her eyes popped open.

"Yours is a rare one." Mamaw nodded. "It took me a while to find it. But yes, two others had it. I marked the page." She pointed to the tiny red ribbon poking out near the beginning of the book.

Bone eagerly flipped the pages open to the spot. The handwriting was incredibly tiny and tidy. Bone could just make out the date at the top: July 31, 1822. Touching the ink, she could see a young woman with long brown hair in an old-timey dress sitting at this same table, only with an oil lamp. She had a cat, too. The entry said, *Tested Olivia today. She didn't appear to have a Gift for animals, plants, weather, or even water. I almost despaired until she touched her deceased grandfather's pocket watch. Olivia described his death back in Scotland in vivid detail, details I'd never divulged to anyone living.*

"She's talking about your Great-great-grandmother Olivia." Mamaw flipped the pages to where the handwriting changed into a beautiful, flowing script with many little illustrations, mostly of objects. "She used her Gift to read objects folks brought her."

"Why would people do that?" Bone gingerly touched a drawing of a rocking horse. She saw a wiry blond woman touching the real rocking horse as she sketched it. Next to the drawing she'd written: *Mrs. Lobelia Smith's son died of cholera on their journey to Virginia from England, March 9, 1834.* Deep sadness radiated off the ink itself.

"To find out something about the owner. Maybe it was a grandfather they never met. A loved one who passed. Or a husband they thought was cheating on them. One fella was even looking for lost treasure." Mamaw tapped an entry marked December 8, 1842. Next to it was a sketch of a treasure map, complete with a big X at the foot of a mountain.

"Really?" Bone squinted as she tried to make out the writing. If she had her druthers, that's the only kind of object she'd touch. "The map was an utter fraud," she read aloud. "Dang."

"Her youngest daughter, Hazel, had the same Gift, too." Mamaw pointed farther down the page. "She moved to Cincinnati with her husband—and opened an antiques store."

"Oh." Bone tried not to sound disappointed, but she was. She couldn't see herself appraising antiques or snooping on affairs or reading dead children's toys for grieving mothers. Finding treasures, yes, but there probably wasn't much call to look for buried gold or silver even now.

"Not everyone puts their Gift to the best use. Your Greatuncle Oakley used his weather sense to scam farmers out west into paying him to make it rain." Mamaw closed up the book and kissed Bone on the forehead. "It's up to you to figure out what to do with yours." She scooped up the ledger. "But do be careful with that damn jar."

Mamaw put the ledger back up on the shelf between the botany and anatomy books. The shelf also held Uncle Ash's veterinary books and a few others. If only she had gotten one of those Gifts, Bone thought. She loved animals, too. Plants maybe not so much. It wasn't fair, though. Mamaw caught Bone staring up at the spines. "Give me a hand with this mess." She waved her in the direction of the elderberries.

～～

Bone helped Mamaw clean up the press and put away the new jars of elderberry syrup on the shelves. Mamaw hummed while each of them thought their own thoughts. Bone was mostly thinking about how in the world she'd make the best use of her Gift. It was a stumper, as Uncle Ash might say.

"How's Ruby?" Mamaw finally asked as she rinsed out the big pot and handed it to Bone to dry.

Bone searched for a good word. "Prickly," she finally said.

Mamaw chuckled.

"Why can't they stay here?" Bone asked. If something happened to Daddy, she would want to come here. "Why do they need to go to Radford?"

"Oh, I offered!" Mamaw ran water through the rubber tubing as she talked. "We could easily build them their own cabin if they

135

wanted. They could help with the garden and the foraging and such." Mamaw hung up the tubing to dry on the pegs over the sink. "But your Aunt Mattie wouldn't hear of it."

Bone wasn't surprised. She couldn't really imagine Mattie living here, even when she was little.

"And I don't blame her. She's always wanted to get out of the country." Mamaw rubbed some minty-smelling ointment into her hands. Bone handed her the dishtowel. "She thought Henry was her ticket out of Big Vein—but he loved it here. She wanted him to get a church in Roanoke or even Richmond."

"What will they do?" Bone recalled the scene Ruby had made over them moving to Radford.

"I expect they'll take Fern and Richard's offer. He can get Mattie on at the powder plant."

"But Ruby doesn't want to go. And she's so angry with Mattie."

"She's grieving her daddy. Both of them are. They'll work things out. Eventually."

"What can I do, Mamaw?"

"Just be Ruby's friend."

Bone thought long and hard about that as she cleaned the press. Ruby had been Bone's friend when it really counted. She tried to stop Mattie from drowning Bone. Ruby had gone for help. And afterward Ruby had sat beside Bone in the rain by the river waiting for the ferry that would never come. The least Bone could do, she figured, was stand beside Ruby when she pulled a prank. Bone knew it was more than that, but it was all she could think to do.

"In that case, can I have some eggs?" Bone asked her grandmother.

"Of course," Mamaw said. "Do I want to know why?"

"Not really," Bone replied. "It's for Halloween, and it'll make Ruby feel better. I hope."

❧

Uncle Ash poked his head in the back door. "Called Lydia, and I got us some trout." He crooked his head toward the area behind the cabin. "Caught them this morning before I made my calls."

"I'll run up to the chicken coop while you help Ash," Mamaw told Bone.

He'd gotten the fire going in the fire pit, a wide ring of bricks dug into the dirt, with a wire grill over part of it. A big cast-iron skillet heated up on one end of the grill. The copper pot for apple butter churning sat off to one side. Wooden chairs ringed the pit. Bone had always loved roasting marshmallows and weenies over this fire with the whole family.

Bone plopped down by the flat counter stone, as she called it. It was just a big flat rock topped with a butcher block. Uncle Ash already had all the fixings for a feast laid out on the block. He cleaned the trout and stuffed them with wild sorrel before laying them gently across the grill. Bone peeled and chopped the potatoes and other vegetables. Mamaw appeared carrying a small basket of eggs and a stick of butter. As she handed the eggs to Bone, Uncle Ash raised an eyebrow. She threw the potatoes, vegetables, mushrooms, and some butter into the skillet. They popped and sizzled, releasing a peppery, woody aroma.

The dogs sprawled in the grass. Overhead, as the stars had begun to peek out, Bone almost sighed. "Tell us a scary story, Uncle Ash," she asked.

"Why don't you tell me one?" he countered as he carefully flipped the trout over on the fire.

He didn't have to ask Bone twice, but she had to think a moment. He knew all the stories she did, mostly because he'd told them to her. Then Bone remembered a Jack ma lantern story Miss Spencer had collected. It wasn't very long. "There once was this fella who was a-coming home on a real dark and foggy night. He got lost right quick. The fog was as thick as peanut butter. He crept along slowly, thinking he was still on the path, but soon he was lost in the woods. Then he spotted a light. He thought it was a neighbor's lantern in the window, so he followed it. Only it never got any closer. He kept walking and walking—plumb right into the swamp, never to be seen again. The light turned out to be a Jack ma lantern."

"He forgot to turn his pockets inside out to keep from being led astray." Uncle Ash slid a piece of crispy trout onto Bone's plate.

"That's hogwash." Mamaw snorted as she passed Bone a big slice of corn bread. "What's wrong, honey?"

Bone had felt the color draining out of her as she finished her story. It was exactly like the dream she'd been having about Daddy. She hoped that he'd turned out his pockets.

15

BONE SUPPRESSED AN enormous yawn the next morning in class. Uncle Ash had gotten her home way past bedtime. Now, Miss Johnson was going on and on about the history of Germany.

Then the mine whistle blew.

It was deep and shrill and cut through everyone in the school, in the whole camp.

Will. Uncle Junior. Bone's mouth went dry. She looked back at Jake and Clay, but they'd already taken off running. Clay's dad was down in the mines, and Jake's was the outside man.

Miss Johnson didn't have to say anything. She opened the door, and everyone else followed her out. Miss Austin was leading the little ones. Outside, adults were walking and running up the road toward the mine.

Uncle Ash pulled up with Mamaw in the passenger seat. Bone, followed a second or two later by Ruby, piled in the back with the dogs, and they peeled up the road. It was a very short yet bumpy trip.

Everyone gathered a distance outside the mine entrance, giving the miners room to work. Ash walked swiftly, cutting his way through the crowd while Mamaw steered Bone and Ruby in his wake. When they got to the front, Bone could see Jake's dad running the mantrip. He gave Jake and Clay a quick hug and shooed them back to the crowd. They found Bone.

"Daddy says it was a cave-in," Jake said between breaths. "Two trapped but they're digging them out."

Clay didn't say a word. He just stared at the mine entrance. Jake put an arm around him.

Mr. Whitaker must be one of them.

Jake nodded his head over toward the mantrip. Marvin Linkous stood there, covered in black with a dusting of ashy powder. He looked like a ghost of himself. He was staring at the mine entrance just like Clay.

Garvin must be the other one.

That meant Uncle Junior and Will were digging them out. A handful of other miners reassured their families. They'd wait around to relieve those doing the digging now.

Bone relaxed, yet felt immediately ashamed. She was relieved it wasn't Junior or Will trapped, but she felt bad about Mr. Whitaker and Garvin. And Marvin was all by himself with no one to comfort him as he waited for word on his twin brother.

Mrs. Linkous pushed her way through the crowd and wrapped Marvin in a tearful hug. Mrs. Kincaid followed her. Marvin made it clear he wasn't going anywhere until Garvin came up. Then he obviously was telling them both what happened. Marvin made digging motions and pointed off in the distance. Will's mother caught Mrs. Linkous's arm to steady her.

Finally, the mantrip jerked into motion, and two ash- and coal-covered figures emerged, one helping the other as he cradled his left arm. The Linkouses and Mrs. Kincaid ran to them. Garvin yelped as his mother squeezed him. Will kissed his mother and headed straight to Clay.

"Daddy?" Clay asked, searching Will's eyes for some clue.

Will dug out his pad, and a pocketful of dirt and ash fell out instead. He mimed digging.

"Clay!" Mrs. Whitaker called as she pushed through the crowd with three little ones in tow.

Mrs. Lilly scooped up the smallest one, Cecilia, who was still in diapers. "Jake!"

Clay and Jake bolted toward their mothers.

"Junior?" Mamaw asked Will.

Will gave her an okay sign.

Bone pointed to him. He nodded and pointed a thumb toward Marvin and Garvin.

"You go take care of them," Bone said.

Will trotted back to the Linkouses, steering them all toward the ambulance.

He really could look after himself and others, with or without a voice.

Still, the waiting was torture.

"Mamaw," Bone asked, "did we do this when Will's daddy died? Stand out here, I mean." Bone had only been a couple years old at the time.

"Yes," Mamaw said with sigh. "I've stood out here all my life."

Bone wondered if her mother could've saved Will's father. The sweater was silent.

ᥫ᭡

About an hour later, the mantrip bumped back up to the surface. Several coal- and ash-covered men gingerly lifted another one out. The ambulance folks loaded him onto a stretcher. Mrs. Whitaker handed the little ones to Clay and Jake, and followed her husband into the ambulance. Jake's mom quickly swooped in and took all of the children under her wing.

A wiry black figure that Bone knew was Junior Reed straightened a kink in his back as he scanned the crowd. Ash waved him over.

Bone had never been so glad Daddy was elsewhere, even if he was in just as dangerous a place. Ruby bolted to hug Junior. She emerged from the bear hug smeared in black.

"Poor baby," Mamaw murmured as she cleaned Ruby's face with a kerchief and a little spit. Then she hugged Junior herself. "I never will get used to this."

"How's Chuck?" Ash asked.

"Lawd, this is the last thing they need," Mamaw said.

First Clay's big brothers went down with their ship in the Pacific. Now his father was hurt or worse.

"He's alive. At least got a broken leg. Garvin's got a busted arm or shoulder." Streaks of sweat ran down Uncle Junior's black and ashy face. He reached his hand out to lean on his brother for a second. "Damn, I'm getting too old for this," He said, wiping his brow with the back of his hand.

"Let's get you home so you can call the girls." Mamaw steered his exhausted body toward the truck. Even over in Radford, Fern and Ivy would've probably heard about the accident by now.

"I'll meet you at the truck. One thing first." Junior walked slowly back over toward the entrance. The ambulance was already speeding away, and families were dispersing with their miners. Nobody bothered to wash up. Grimy, blackened men and boys had smudged their loved ones with their coal-and-ash embraces. Will and his mother were beginning to walk home. Junior stopped them and shook Will's hand. He told Mrs. Kincaid something that made her straighten up and take Will's arm.

Later that evening, after Junior had called his girls, scrubbed himself pink, enjoyed a big supper, and collapsed in his chair by the fire, he was ready to talk about the accident. The story was eerily familiar to Bone.

"Me and Will were blasting a new shaft. Chuck and the twins were taking timbers from an old one. Since we don't have anybody left to run the mill, we get most of our support timbers from played-out shafts. When the mine rumbled, Will took off running toward them, with me on his heels." Uncle Junior shook his head in admiration. He then explained how they found Marvin frantically digging. "He'd been carrying the timbers toward us when the roof caved in on Garvin and Chuck. Marvin didn't want to leave his brother, but Will made him go get help. He pointed and that boy took off. Will then just about single-handedly rescued Garvin." He looked at Bone. "Your Will crawled right in there and cut Garvin loose where he was pinned. After that, it took the rest of us digging for an hour or so to reach Chuck." Uncle Junior sank back in his chair.

Mamaw passed Junior a cup of coffee.

"Uncle Junior, what did you tell Will and his mom?"

"That I was damn proud of him. And that William would've been proud, too. If that young man could talk, he'd be quite a supervisor someday, or anything else he set his mind to. Those boys would follow him anywhere." Junior sighed.

"He could still work the mines the rest of his life, couldn't he?" Bone asked. "He loves the work." Even as she said this,

Bone thought of Mr. Whitaker getting carted away in an ambulance.

"I know." Junior blew on his still-steaming coffee. "Only I don't know how long these mines will hold out."

"What do you mean?" Bone had never considered that something might happen to the mines. The miners, yes, but not the mines themselves. Then Bone remembered Uncle Junior's Gift. She'd never seen him using it, or even heard him talk about it. "Did your Gift show you this? How does it work?"

"Yes and no. If I put my hand on a vein of coal and concentrate, I can see a map in my head of how it runs. Lately, the veins are petering out—or they go way too deep for us to get at with pick and shovel." He straightened up in his chair and looked at Bone. "Even if it weren't my Gift, I know there's only so much coal in the ground around here. I wouldn't be surprised if these mines get played out in a few more years. It's already happening at Great Valley."

"What would you do if it did?" Bone asked.

"Oh, I could go to work at the powder plant or another factory in the area. Or I could help Ash and Mother farm. Your daddy and me talked about building houses—once folks had money again." Uncle Junior yawned mightily. "Or maybe I could retire by then. I think we all got at least until after the war." Uncle Junior closed his eyes. "And we're gonna dig as much as we can for the war effort."

Mamaw gently took the cup from his hand.

Bone sat on the hearth and pondered. So far war had killed Uncle Henry, the Whitaker brothers, baseball, and now maybe the coal mines.

Daddy could do all of those things Junior mentioned and more if the coal ran out. But Will probably couldn't do any of them—not without a voice. Will needed his voice—and as crazy as it sounded, that jelly jar had it. Bone had to warn Will not to use the jelly jar.

And Bone needed to figure out how to get his voice out. She had to touch it.

16

THE EVENING WAS right airish. It was only a few days until Halloween, and Bone hated that it got darker earlier and earlier each day. The headlights of an approaching truck danced in the woods like ghost lights. Bone pulled her butter-yellow sweater around her tight and dashed to the Kincaids'.

Bone rapped on their door. It was late, but the lights were still on in the front room.

Will opened the door.

"You okay?" Bone plunged her hands in her pockets.

Will nodded.

"We need to talk about the jar." Bone whispered the last part.

Will ducked back inside and emerged with his coat on. He patted the lump in the pocket. He pointed toward the boardinghouse. Bone understood. He didn't want his mother to hear.

They sat on the back porch of the boardinghouse in their usual spots on the steps, the jar between them. Will pushed it toward her.

"Mamaw says we shouldn't mess with it anymore." Bone pulled her sweater tight around her.

Will put his hand over the jar.

"It's stealing sounds!" she blurted out. "Uncle Ash said Mr. Childress's dogs lost their voices."

Will put the jar back in his pocket and pulled out his notebook. Then he scribbled out something.

I know. Figured it out after the crickets.

"Crickets?" Then Bone remembered that night on the back porch. The crickets had gone silent. "Oh! Why didn't you tell me?"

Will shrugged.

"You knew it was stealing sounds!" Bone leapt up and faced him.

He nodded without looking at her. *I've been real careful*, he wrote.

"You need to stop!"

Will shook his head. He wrote furiously and shoved the note into her hand. *I ain't caught nothing new since the ballgame.*

He wrote some more. *And I listen only where it's real quiet.*

"You mean at the cemetery."

Will glared at her. Then he nodded.

Bone paced up and down in front of Will for a couple moments. "That dang jar stole a bunch of sounds ever since your daddy died holding it." She let that sink in.

Will gawped at her. Then he scribbled out: *How do you know that?*

Bone sat down beside him again. "Uncle Junior said so. They found your daddy with that jar in his hand. Must be why it's got power."

Will pulled the jar out of his pocket and slid it over to her once more.

I'll stop—if you read the jar.

"He died with that thing in his hand." Bone pointed to the jar. "Do you really want to hear about *that?*" She didn't want to see more than she already had.

I need to know everything.

"Oh, dang it," Bone muttered. She took a deep breath, grabbed the jar, and closed her eyes.

What do you need to show me?

The jar was warm like an ember to the touch, but it didn't burn her. Instead it pulled at her, like it wanted to embrace her. She saw Will Sr. sitting in the mine, only the light of his mining lamp—and Mr. Scott's next to him—illuminating the lunch spread in front of him. It was dark as it was now. Between them, they had a small picnic of fried chicken, dill pickles, and white bread, slathered with apple butter, spread out on their kerchiefs. Mr. Scott was talking about football. Mr. Kincaid scraped the jelly jar clean, licking it for good measure. Then he leaned back against the wall of coal and daydreamed about picking apples in the summertime, birds chirping overhead, cicadas whirring in the distance, and little Will at his side, jabbering away. Both of them laughed at the four-year-old's bad jokes.

Will elbowed Bone slightly. She explained what she was seeing. "You told some terrible jokes." Will chuckled.

He loved apples and apple butter, Will wrote.

"He loved you, silly." And he missed the summer and the sunshine. Bone recognized the feeling of longing. She dove a bit deeper. She could feel a wave of longing washing over her. Will's dad was longing for the sunny days in the orchard, swimming and fishing in the river, and, most of all, time spent with his boy. Then the mine rumbled and the timbers above them cracked. A rock fell, and the roof collapsed around William and Scotty. Bone felt dark, cold, and hollow.

"*William!*" Scotty yelled. It sounded a million miles away.

Mr. Kincaid uttered a muffled reply. Inside, she could feel him screaming, but the screams stayed bottled up, unable to get out. He spit out dirt and ash as best he could. And he was still holding the jelly jar. A burning, gnawing hunger radiated off it.

Will's dad filled that jar with his longing—for all the things he was going to miss. Apple orchards. River. Baseball. Trains. Laughter. Sarah. And most of all, Will. Hearing his jokes. Seeing him grow up. Teaching him to hit a ball. Watching him graduate. Get a job. Have kids of his own. The wave of longing was so strong, Bone could barely breathe. It was crushing. She almost dropped the jar.

"*I love you, son,*" William managed to whisper into the jar. The world went black—except for the ember of longing burning in the jelly jar in his hand.

Bone set the jar down gently between her and Will.

Will snatched it back.

Bone felt like crying, but the tears wouldn't come. Will's daddy poured all his love and longing into that glass jar—and he loved Will so much . . . so much that it made Bone jealous and ashamed of that jealousy. And even a bit angry. She whispered what she'd seen.

Will sat there mutely.

"Say something," Bone whispered.

He opened his mouth, and nothing came out.

All that, and Will still couldn't talk. Her Gift was useless.

Bone dashed into the house, feeling hollowed out yet burning inside.

BONE TOSSED AND turned in bed, thinking about Will's dad—and her own. She'd had the nightmare again where Daddy was wandering through cold, dark woods, lost. This time, he only had the light of a Jack o'lantern to show him the way home. Or was it a jelly jar? Or was he following a Jack ma lantern into the swamps? Somewhere in the dream, one thing had turned into another and another. And the big iron gates of heaven and hell had swung shut on him.

Bone stared at the cracks in the bedroom ceiling. She did not want to go back to sleep. How did Will's voice get into the jar in the first place? Would she have to read the jar again to find out? Or had his mother seen something? Bone sat up. Was that what Mrs. Kincaid hadn't wanted to say?

The clock on her bedside table said it was only 9:30 p.m. Mrs. Kincaid might still be up.

Bone threw on her dungarees and sweater, grabbed her boots, and crept down the back stairs of the boardinghouse. Someone was still listening to the radio in the parlor, Uncle Junior by the sound of the snoring. Bone tiptoed out the back door and slipped on her boots.

The lights still burned bright at the Kincaids'—and Mrs. Kincaid sat on the porch, knitting and rocking.

Bone's boots crunched on the dry ground as she approached.

"Is that you, Will?" Mrs. Kincaid stood up.

"No, ma'am," Bone said, coming into the light of the porch. "He's not here?"

Mrs. Kincaid tossed her knitting down beside the chair. "No, and he keeps coming home later and later. I thought he might be doing something he ought not to with you, but Mrs. Price assured me you were in bed promptly at 8:30 every night." She looked suspiciously at Bone.

"I couldn't sleep." Bone couldn't imagine what Mrs. Kincaid thought she might be doing with Will. But that didn't matter. Bone knew where he was: the cemetery. "I'm worried about him, too." Bone walked up the steps of the Kincaid porch. "But I know where he is."

"Where, young lady?" Mrs. Kincaid stood, hands on hips, towering over Bone.

"The cemetery. Talking to his daddy," Bone added softly.

Mrs. Kincaid gawped for a moment and then crumpled back into her rocking chair like the air had gone right out of her. "The cemetery," she muttered in disbelief.

"Why did you give his father's dinner bucket to Uncle Junior?" Bone asked as kindly as she could.

Mrs. Kincaid looked at her strangely. Finally, she spoke. "I found Will playing with his daddy's gear after the funeral. He was talking to his daddy and telling him knock-knock jokes." Her voice caught. "I just couldn't bear to watch it. Couldn't bear to have the dinner bucket especially in the house. So I asked Junior to get rid of it. Scotty was still in the hospital at the time, or I woulda asked him."

Bone had seen a flash of Will in his Sunday best talking and holding the jar. Now Bone could see clearly what had happened. Will had told his joke into the jar at the wake. And his mama gave away the jar.

"Did Will stop talking right after that?" Bone asked. She already knew the answer, though.

Mrs. Kincaid considered it. "Yes, he did. I never heard him utter another word after that. At first, I thought he was mad at me for giving away the gear. But the doctor said it was grief. And maybe he'd grow out of it."

Mrs. Kincaid picked up her knitting again, but she just stared at the needles like she'd forgotten how to work them.

Will wasn't going to grow out of it. That crazy jar had captured his voice. That's why just reading it didn't help. Bone was stumped, though, about what to do. How was her Gift supposed to solve this?

18

IT WAS HALLOWEEN at last. Bone didn't know how to help Will, but at least she could be there for Ruby and Clay. And she had eggs. First, though, they had to collect tin cans for the 4-H scrap drive. Between houses, Bone told Ruby and the boys that she was in. The boys whooped in delight. Ruby merely cracked a smile. She whispered a thank-you as they knocked on the next door. They stopped at every house in Big Vein except the parsonage.

Later, when Uncle Junior was snoring away in his room, Bone slunk down the back stairs, boots in one hand and a sack of old eggs in another. She laced up her boots on the porch, and then took off running toward the parsonage. It was almost 10 o'clock.

Jake and Clay jumped out of the bushes and about gave her a heart attack. "Is this it?" she whispered. She'd expected the whole school the way Jake had talked.

"They'll be along directly," Clay assured her—or himself, more likely—as he glanced up the road.

Three figures came creeping alongside the parsonage. Giggles escaped from Pearl and Opal. Ruby whirled on them with a sharp hiss. They fell in meekly behind her.

Each had a few eggs in hand. They scrunched down behind the azalea bush across the road and counted up all of the eggs. They had fewer than a dozen between them. Some were rottener than others.

Pearl couldn't help giggling, and Opal didn't want to throw any eggs, so Ruby glared at both of them. "You're useless," she muttered, sounding every inch her mother. The Little Jewels looked crushed.

"Why don't you two keep an eye on the road," Bone whispered. "Pearl, you head up yonder. Opal, down there. Let us know if anybody is coming."

Pearl and Opal mouthed their thank-yous at Bone and took off.

"Useless," Ruby muttered again. She handed the boys and Bone their share of the eggs.

Jake nudged Bone. "You get the honor of the first throw."

Ruby and Clay nodded.

"She about killed you," Ruby reminded her. Again.

For a second, Bone thought she spied a light at the edge of Flat Woods. *Foxfire,* she told herself. *Only foxfire.*

She turned to face the parsonage. Again, it was sealed up tighter than a pickle jar. Bone stood there, her arm cocked and ready to hurl an egg. She could still taste the cold iron of that bathwater Mattie almost drowned her in. Aunt Mattie was why Mama died. No, Mama picked Aunt Mattie over her and Daddy. And Daddy chose the war over Bone. She couldn't move. A red-hot chunk of coal ate at her gut. Still, she was stuck there, unable to throw the stupid egg.

"Oh, for Pete's sake," Ruby said, taking the egg from Bone's hand. She rifled it at the front door. The egg splatted against the wood. Ruby fired another and then another. She painted the crisp white door and siding in yellow. Bone handed her more eggs; so did the boys.

"She's a regular Cy Young," Clay whispered in appreciation.

Ruby hurled those eggs with astounding ferocity and accuracy. She hit the door five times as well as the front window with the gold star. Once.

Jake handed her the last of the eggs. By then, the tears were streaming down Ruby's face.

The front door swung open. "What in the blue blazes is going on . . ." Aunt Mattie had a shotgun in her hand.

Splat. Ruby hit her mama square in the face with the last egg.

The boys dove down behind the bushes. Jake pulled Bone down, too.

"Remind me to pick her next time we play ball," Jake said. Clay stifled a laugh. Bone peered around the bush to see what was happening. "Get down here!" she called to Ruby. "She's got a gun!"

"Oh, it ain't loaded!" Ruby said loudly. She scooped up a rock and threw it at the window, like she was aiming for the gold star. The glass shattered. "Daddy didn't allow shot in the house."

"Ruby Louise Albert!" Mattie dropped the shotgun. It wasn't loaded. Her mouth gaped open. Then she closed it into a hard line. "Did that cousin of yours put you up to this?"

"Bone?" Ruby closed the distance between her and her mother as she talked. "She wouldn't even throw one egg! And you pert near killed her!" Ruby scooped up another rock. "You brought this on yourself. You killed everyone's fun. And you killed Daddy." She threw the rock; it went sailing through the broken window. "You drove him away!"

Bone stood up. She couldn't believe the words coming out of Ruby's mouth.

"Damn," Clay said. The boys rose to their feet, too.

Aunt Mattie was as white as a ghost. And silent. Ruby kept yelling and throwing things. Mattie stood there and took it.

Lights flickered on up and down the road, and sleepy folks stood on their porches—then quickly went back inside. The boys and the Little Jewels slunk off to their own houses.

Bone couldn't look away, let alone move. She watched. Ruby let it all out, all that hurt and fear and rage she'd been keeping bottled up inside since she stopped talking to Aunt Mattie. And even before that. When Bone had touched the gold star, she could feel Ruby holding back, keeping a lid on her feelings. The lid wasn't on too tight, though. The anger and pain leaked out in little ways, in little fights, but never saying what she really felt deep down. Now, it all flowed out, a furious river of words.

"I wish it'd been you instead of Daddy," Ruby spit out. She was standing right in Mattie's face. Then she crumpled to the ground, the hot air and fury gone out of her. Ruby started crying. Mattie swayed there.

Bone started toward Ruby, but Aunt Mattie reached down and tenderly pulled Ruby to her feet. Bone stopped as Mattie wrapped her arms around Ruby, rocking her back and forth.

"I didn't mean it, Mama," Ruby sniffled.

"I know," Mattie murmured. They both stood and cried a bit, holding each other tightly, before they made their way back into the house.

Bone felt a hollow burning ache watching them.

Mamaw had said jars are like people, keeping things bottled up. And things went bad if you didn't let them out. *Is that why Will doesn't talk? Is he mad at his father for dying?*

Yes and no, Bone reckoned. It was more complicated than that. Will's voice was in that jar.

Bone thought on it as she walked back toward the boarding-house. If he broke the jar, he'd free his voice. Bone was sure of it. He needed to hurl that thing and smash it into bits, just like Ruby had shattered that window.

Only, he'd never do that. He was obsessed with that dad-blame jar.

Bone sank onto the back steps in the dark. The yard was still and quiet, and everyone in the house was long in bed. Not even a cricket chirped.

Would it work if *she* broke the jelly jar?

She had a niggling feeling it wouldn't.

Bone closed her eyes and asked her Gift what to do. The images she'd seen when she touched the jar came flooding back. The darkness. The jar glowing like a lantern. Mr. Kincaid's dying hand wrapped around it. Will's daddy poured all his longing and love into that jar—for Will. It was his jar and his to break.

Will had to get angry, really angry, like Ruby did. Only, Bone had never seen Will get mad. He was always as cool as the river on a hot summer's day.

She'd have to do something pretty low to make him erupt.

19

COME SUNDAY, MRS. PRICE sent Bone on to church alone. Nobody mentioned the egging incident. Mattie and Ruby both sat puffy-eyed in their usual spots. The 4-H Club had collected a truckload of tin cans, which Uncle Ash was running over to the ballpark. Uncle Junior was fixing the parsonage window during the service.

Bone slipped a note into Will's pocket after church. *Meet me at the cemetery. Bring it.*

Bone sat on the stone bench by William A. Kincaid Sr.'s grave. And she waited. She wondered what she'd learn if she touched the headstones. Probably just something about the man who carved them. Finally, Will trudged up the path. He warily handed her the jar.

She had to be sure of a few things first. Closing her eyes, she opened the jar and felt its stories spill out. The train, the dogs, Charlie McCarthy, and a few others she hadn't heard before. And there it was. One very small voice telling a knock-knock joke.

How did you get in the jar? she asked.

A small Will in his Sunday best sat with his daddy's mining gear. Adult voices murmured in the background. The dinner bucket was dented. Will pried off the lid and found the jelly jar. He unscrewed the jar. His father's voice lilted out, saying he loved Will. Will whispered a joke back to his father. His voice was as full of longing as his daddy's: longing to have his father home, longing to be like him. He screwed the jar lid on tight—right before his mother snatched it out of his hands. Bone screwed the lid back on tight, too.

Will Sr. had poured all of his hopes and wishes into the jar. He would've chosen to stay with Will, if he could.

Unlike Mama.

Bone pushed the thought aside and focused on the jar again. One more thing.

Does Will need to be the one to break you?

She knew the answer, but she needed to be sure.

She saw young Will again, pouring his five-year-old love and grief into the jar and sealing it up tight. Then she saw new images. An older Will knelt at the graveside opening the jar again and again. He was reliving that moment of his father's death every time he opened the jar. Neither the jar nor Will was letting it out for good. Will had to be the one who set it all free.

Will tugged gently at her sweater. He'd sat down beside her while she'd communed with the jar again.

"Will, you need to break this jar," Bone told him.

Will looked stricken. He tried to snatch the jar away from her. She wouldn't let him. She stood on the bench with the jar over her head. He still could've easily gotten it from her. Instead, he wrote something out.

I can't. It's all I have of Daddy. His voice.

He'd spent hours on end listening to that voice.

"Your daddy wanted so many things for you!" she said. "He'd want you to have your voice back!"

Will shook his head.

I'd lose his.

Bone sighed. She'd really hoped she wouldn't have to do this. What if it didn't work? What if it did? What if he wouldn't break it? *Foller your own lights.* They—and her Gift—were telling her this was the only way.

Bone took a deep, deep breath. "What else was on your list? Baseball. Trains. My stories?" She unscrewed the lid, and even as the sounds played out, she started in on a story, "Fill, Bowl, Fill."

"Once there was a . . ."

Will staggered back as he realized what she was doing.

Then he dove for the jar.

Bone shielded it with her body while she screwed the lid back on. She mouthed the words "the end" as she handed the jar to Will. She jumped off the bench, backing away, and stood on the path.

Fury mounted in Will's eyes as he glowered wordlessly at her and the jar. He stalked back and forth in front of his father's grave, blazing at her and then his father, a silent argument with himself building up inside.

Will kicked over the bench. Puffs of dirt rose around it.

Then he whipped around and smashed the jar against the tombstone.

The sounds of the jar, including her story, rose through the air around him like ghost lights and flitted off into the woods. There they echoed among the trees, the baying dogs chasing the rest up the mountain into the shadows.

"How could you?" Will hollered, his voice raspy from long silence. "You had no right!"

He spewed long-unused words at her. Bone took it. He'd obviously learned some new ones down in the mines. But she took it.

Then he turned to the headstone. "How could you?" he raged. He yelled at his father for leaving them, for leaving Mama to scrub floors, for him having to leave school. Will's voice was much deeper than Bone had expected. He went on until he ran out of words. For now. He collapsed on the ground beside her.

"Feel better?" Bone asked.

"Yes," Will said, resting his head in his hands. He looked as tired as he had after that first day mining. "Give me a minute," he added. Then he mimed that he'd clean up the glass. Will would have to get used to talking again.

Bone nodded. She wrapped the butter-yellow sweater around herself and turned toward the back row of the cemetery.

She had a bone to pick with Mama.

Bone stepped over the rows of Scotts and Prices to her mother's grave. She stood there for a long moment, not knowing where to begin and even feeling a bit stupid. Yet that white-hot ember burned in her gut. She glanced back at Will. He was talking—out loud—to his father. When she looked at her mother's grave, Daddy's words kept coming back to her. *She's not there.*

But that was the problem. "You're not here," she said aloud. She said it again and again, a little louder each time until she burst right open. "Daddy's run off to the war, and he left me with Aunt Mattie," she hollered. "Even if he didn't get himself drafted, he'd'a joined up. He's off saving the world instead of being here with me. And you chose to save Mattie instead of being here with me." Bone could feel hot tears, rising over the dam inside her. The pressure, spilling, bursting through. She fought it down. "And all I got was this stupid thing!" Bone yanked at the sleeve of her mother's butter-yellow sweater. As soon as she touched it, though, she saw her mother laying the sweater over Mattie. Mama poured all her love and longing into it. All this love was for her sister? The one who'd caused her death? Mama chose Mattie, not her.

But then Mama whispered, *"For Bone. Give this to Bone."* She sank back into the chair and slipped away.

The fire went right out of Bone. She didn't fight back the tears this time. Mama had loved her as much as Will's daddy loved him. She didn't know why she'd doubted it. She hugged herself in the sweater. The butter-yellow yarn was as full of love and longing as the jelly jar.

Mama loved her.

She dropped to her knees. Tears flooded out as she cried a river that almost quenched that ember burning inside her. Almost.

At last, Bone wiped her eyes on Mama's butter-yellow sweater.

And it took it.

20

BONE BRUSHED THE dirt off her knees and dried her eyes on Mama's butter-yellow sweater.

She made her way back to the path. There, Uncle Ash was helping Will right the bench. Corolla lifted his leg against it when they were done.

"I swear, dog." Uncle Ash shook his head. "You all right, Forever Girl?"

Bone shrugged and wiped her nose on her sleeve. She ached like a wrung-out dishrag, but her insides no longer burned.

"Y'all been up here a while." Uncle Ash put an arm around her. "Mama sent me to find you."

He walked Bone and Will back to the boardinghouse.

Will stayed silent. She guessed he wasn't ready yet to speak to someone else, even if it was only Uncle Ash. To her surprise, the boardinghouse was full of people. Mamaw and Mrs. Price had organized a belated Halloween party.

The parlor smelled of apple cider and pumpkin pies. The dining table was laden with pie, cookies, homemade candies, and punch. Apples bobbed in a tub of water in the corner.

Ruby entered carrying a tray of candy apples. "Mama sends her regrets, but she had to run over to Radford this afternoon. She got a job!" Ruby beamed. "She's looking at an apartment for us."

Uncle Junior brought in pumpkins for carving. Mamaw handed Bone a purple candy she'd made. It tasted of elderberry and honey.

All the kids from school were there. Clay and Jake were dressed like skeletons. Others were dressed like cowboys, ghosts, and clowns—whatever they could create at the last minute from old clothes or sheets. Mrs. Price handed Bone a witch's hat and cape she'd made out of burlap and dyed black. Hester Prynne rubbed up against Bone as she donned them.

After the pumpkin carving and bobbing for apples, the boys called to her to tell a story.

"Not too scary, though," Clay said as he pulled his little sister, Cecilia, onto his lap. "How about that Stingy Jack one again?"

Bone settled on a slightly different version this time. A good storyteller never told a story the same way twice, Uncle Ash always said. She whispered something to Will, and he went to stand by the light switch. She gathered up her props—one of the Jack o'lanterns, a candle, and a book of matches—and turned Uncle Junior's chair by the hearth to face the audience as they all settled down on the rug.

"Once there was an old boy named Jack, and he loved to play tricks on folks." Bone winked at Clay as she plopped into the big chair. "People called him Stingy Jack on account of how miserly he was.

"One day, Stingy Jack run across this old man lying on the ground outside his cabin. Jack took him home and fed him. Only it turned out to be the devil in disguise. And he wanted Jack's soul." Bone explained how Jack tricked the devil into turning into a coin and then not taking his soul. This time. Ten years later he came back. "Now Jack said he'd go with the devil if he fetched him an apple from that tree. The devil climbed up the apple tree, but Jack quick-like carved crosses in the trunk of the tree, trapping the devil once again. This time he agreed to never collect Jack's soul if he'd just let him down."

One of the little kids laughed with delight.

"When Jack died, though, Saint Peter didn't want him. And when Jack went down to the other place, the devil said a bargain was a bargain. He didn't want him there anyways."

Bone paused for effect.

"So what was Jack supposed to do?" Clay's little sister asked.

"That's what he asked the devil," Bone answered. "'It's so cold and dark out,' Jack said."

Will flipped the lights off, and the young ones screeched and giggled.

Bone struck a match and lit the small candle in her hand. "'Since you did me a kindness, feeding me and taking me into your house, I'll do you one in return,' the devil said. Then he nipped off to the fires of damnation and fetched Jack an ember. He tossed it to him. 'To light your way.'"

Bone put the candle in the Jack o'lantern. Its orange light flickered in the darkness.

"Jack scooped up the ember and carved out a pumpkin to carry the light in." She picked up the Jack o'lantern and made it bob around the room, to more squeals and giggles. "And ever since, Jack has roamed the earth carrying that light in a pumpkin. People see the light from his lantern bobbing around in the woods and out in graveyards, especially around Halloween. Sometimes people follow the light, getting terribly lost in the mountains. So we light our own lanterns and leave out treats to scare away Jack . . ."

Bone handed the Jack o'lantern to Will, and he said the words "the end."

The crowd gasped.

Author's Note:
Story Sources

Like Bone, I love Halloween and its stories. In *Lingering Echoes*, Bone delights in telling the tale of "Stingy Jack." It's an origin story for the custom of carving Jack o'lanterns as well as for legends of mysterious lights that lead people astray. In my research— and I do not claim to be an expert in folklore—I found this tale in popular sources, such as on the History Channel, in newspaper and magazine stories, and on storytelling/Appalachian blogs. All claim "Stingy Jack" is an Irish folktale. (I have no reason to doubt this, but I don't have a scholarly source for this story.)

The Irish folktale is very similar to the Appalachian story "Wicked John and the Devil." Folklorist Richard Chase collected this story and published it in *Grandfather Tales*. Both the Irish and Appalachian versions involve a wicked man who tricks the devil and ends up roaming the earth with a burning lump of coal—in a carved turnip or pumpkin. Chase actually changed the protagonist's name from Jack to John to avoid confusion with the younger, non-wicked Jack of the Jack Tales. The differences between the Irish and American versions lie mainly in the methods Jack uses to trick Satan into not taking his soul. "Wicked John and the Devil" is also a bit more convoluted, complicating the plot with three wishes and several dim-witted sons of the devil. It's a great story, but I chose to use the Irish version for simplicity's sake! You can read more about the Appalachian version and its sources on Ferrum College's Appalachian Literature site (http://www2.ferrum.edu/applit/).

By the way, the haunted mirror that Uncle Ash mentions is a local ghost story. In Radford, Virginia, La Riviere mansion—also called Ingles Castle—is supposedly haunted by a lady in the mirror. The mansion—a Queen Anne structure that does look like a castle—was built in 1892 by William Ingles. A family friend, Anne McClanahan Bass (aka Aunt Nannie), was standing by a mirror in the parlor when lightning struck nearby. Like a photograph, the mirror captured her likeness. (Mirrors have silver nitrate in them, and that substance was actually used in photography at the time.) After her death, Aunt Nannie's presence was reportedly felt in the castle.

Oh, and the fairy stones can really be found at Fairy Stone State Park in Patrick County, Virginia. The Civilian Conservation Corps built the park and lake in the early 1930s. To learn more about the stones and the legend behind them, please check out the Virginia State Parks website (http://www.dcr.virginia.gov/state-parks/blog/legend-of-the-fairy-stone).